How could Elizabeth get involved with that commitmentphobic slacker?

Sam wasn't one of those guys who was a jerk in disguise—he was totally open about it and unapologetic! Yeah, Jessica knew Sam was really good-looking and had his deep moments. And yeah, he and Elizabeth had a long history. But after the stuff he'd pulled on Elizabeth two months ago? How *could* she?

Elizabeth finally emerged from the shower, a towel around her. "Jessica, I'm not going to defend Sam right now, okay? I know this seems really sudden. Especially after the past couple of months. But trust me—I know what I'm doing."

"So you *are* getting involved with Sam?"

Jessica would have preferred a teeth cleaning to the sparkle that appeared in Elizabeth's eyes the minute she said Sam's name.

Bantam Books in the Sweet Valley University series.
Ask your bookseller for the books you have missed.

And don't miss these Sweet Valley
University Thriller Editions:

Visit the Official Sweet Valley Web Site on the Internet at:
http://www.sweetvalley.com

SWEET VALLEY UNIVERSITY®

Elizabeth in Love

Written by
Laurie John

Created by
FRANCINE PASCAL

BANTAM BOOKS
NEW YORK · TORONTO · LONDON · SYDNEY · AUCKLAND

RL: 8, AGES 014 AND UP

ELIZABETH IN LOVE
A Bantam Book / July 2000

Sweet Valley High® and Sweet Valley University®
are registered trademarks of Francine Pascal.
Conceived by Francine Pascal.

Produced by 17th Street Productions,
an Alloy Online, Inc. company.
33 West 17th Street
New York, NY 10011.

ISBN: 0-553-49347-7

Visit us on the Web! www.randomhouse.com/teens

Published simultaneously in the United States and Canada

Bantam Books is an imprint of Random House Children's Books, a
division of Random House, Inc. BANTAM BOOKS and the rooster
colophon are registered trademarks of Random House, Inc. Bantam Books,
1540 Broadway, New York, New York 10036.

PRINTED IN THE UNITED STATES OF AMERICA

OPM   0 9 8 7 6 5 4 3 2 1

To Serenity Lopez

Chapter One

Either Sam Burgess is lying next to me in my bed, or I'm having the dream of my life, Elizabeth Wakefield thought.

She looked up at the ceiling, counted to ten, then looked to her left again.

It was no dream. That was definitely Sam—half covered by her blue-and-white flowered comforter—sprawled next to her. That was *his* rock-hard chest rising and falling with each sleeping breath under a black T-shirt, which had tangled up around his waist to reveal his six-pack abs. Those were *his* faded Levi's perfectly fitting his slim hips and long legs . . . *his* sandy brown shock of silky hair, *his* long, light brown eyelashes, *his* perfect face. . . . Yes, that was definitely Sam Burgess in bed with her.

If she wasn't looking right at him, even she

wouldn't believe it. But late last night Sam—Elizabeth's obsession, nemesis, and housemate since last September—had come upstairs to her room to hash out their problems finally.

He hadn't left.

She shook her head in disbelief. For almost the entire time they had known each other, they had been at each other's throats. How had they gone from a pair of Ultimate Fighting Champions to *Dawson's Creek* territory?

Elizabeth smiled. Before last night she and Sam had been barely speaking. It was just last week that they'd begun acknowledging each other's presence for the first time in two months. They'd ignored each other completely. If he was in the kitchen, she'd go without breakfast. If he was in the living room hogging the television, she'd listen to the radio in her attic bedroom instead. Anything to avoid being within the same five feet of him.

And with good reason. He'd hurt her terribly two months ago. She'd dared to mistake an unexpected kiss for actually meaning something, and he'd freaked out in typical Sam fashion and taken off, unable to deal with the whole thing. She'd finally tracked him down—in a ritzy hotel he himself owned, where he'd been shacked up in the lap of luxury with his (platonic) friend Anna. At the time, though, Elizabeth, like everyone else, had thought Sam was poverty-stricken. She'd also thought that Anna was another of Sam's conquests. Elizabeth had never felt so betrayed in her life. Sam had tried to explain, but how could she have listened to a word he said? Both angry and hurt, they'd avoided each other. Until last night.

Last night he'd been ready to tell her everything, and she'd been ready to listen. But instead they'd kissed. For hours. And hours. And apparently had eventually fallen asleep, still fully dressed. Elizabeth glanced down at her baggy sweats and old, faded tank top. *Really sexy,* she thought with a smile.

Sam was an amazing kisser. But then again, Elizabeth had already known that from when they'd briefly hooked up last summer. *Wow,* Elizabeth thought, a small yawn escaping her. *It's now May, which means Sam and I met for the first time almost an entire* year *ago.* A lot had happened in that year.

Like my sophomore year at SVU, she thought, recalling all the plans she'd made for herself back in September. Plans to loosen up, not be so serious and rigid. Well, wasn't the fact that she and Sam were lying next to each other a very good indication that she'd made good on her promises to herself?

3

Speaking of promises, a vision of the hefty manila envelope she'd mailed just last week to the University of Boston floated into her mind. Elizabeth gnawed on her lower lip. She'd been a bit too impulsive. But at the time the scholarship contest she'd entered had seemed like a lifeline. She'd seen a flyer for the University of Boston's prestigious Visiting Student Writer program; if you were chosen, you spent an entire semester at U of B, taking two independent studies, critiquing creative-writing students, and giving three readings of your own work. Last week the thought of leaving Sam, SVU, and her other two unsupportive housemates for the fall semester of her junior year had sounded perfect.

But now . . .

She'd just forget about it. She probably wouldn't win anyway. The University of Boston was a really good school, and the Visiting Student Writer program was incredibly competitive.

Sam stirred. Elizabeth burrowed down, sneaking a glance at the clock. Five-thirty. Plenty of time before they had to get up. She felt like she had swallowed a crate of ginger ale, she was so nervous and excited. Finally it had happened. She was finished denying her feelings for him, and Sam was obviously finished with running away from his feelings for her.

4

And she knew the perfect way to celebrate their new relationship: by attending SVU's spring semi-formal next Friday night. Did Sam even own a tuxedo? she wondered. The thought made her laugh. She doubted that very much. But he'd sure look good in the one he'd rent for the occasion.

Crash.

Todd Wilkins looked up in dismay as the door to his apartment knocked over a towering heap of pizza boxes, beer cans, and empty plastic bottles of Pepsi, sending the cans rolling all over his teeny linoleum kitchen floor.

"Dammit!" Todd yelled, kicking a path into the kitchen and sitting down at the kitchen table. In his hand were three envelopes that bore his handwriting and return address: replies for all the summer internships he'd applied for in Sweet Valley.

Todd rubbed his eyes and yawned deeply, cracking open a can of Pepsi and swigging half in one mouthful. These late nights at Frankie's were killers. When he'd first started out, he'd pictured himself like an actor in a movie: the jukebox pumping, pretty girls at the bar, pouring drinks like a pro, wiping off the bar with a rag, giving people advice, and smoking a cigarette—no hands, just like Clint Eastwood. But in reality

5

the work came in two flavors: tiring and boring.

First of all, as assistant manager of Frankie's Bar, he had to keep an eye on all of the servers—make sure they weren't overpouring, serving too many free drinks, hanging around gabbing on the phone in back, or chatting with friends at their tables. Not too easy when *another* big part of his job was to stay on the good side of the servers, who could either make or break his evening in terms of customer satisfaction. After all, it was *him* the customer yelled for when his waitress wouldn't give him another drink or told him that the men's room was on the other side of Frankie's and that they were currently banging around looking for a urinal in the ladies'.

Also, there was another big part of the job Todd hadn't counted on when he'd eagerly accepted the promotion from back-bar guy to assistant manager: the responsibility. Sure, the ability to pay his own rent solo, drink a beer whenever he wanted, and have his days free had seemed great when he was a student, but actually, being a real, live workingman made his days as a student seem like some Sweet Valley version of *The Real World*. Counting up the till each night in the early morning hours, handling the scheduling for a pack of moody servers, knowing that keeping order in a bar full of hard-drinking guys, businesspeople, and construction workers was all on his shoulders sometimes made him feel like he was going to stagger—even collapse—under the load.

Welcome back from Fantasy Island, Todd, he could almost hear his parents saying. *We'll give you back the keys to the BMW—when you stop making Beavis look like the next Bill Gates.*

That's why he was so excited about these internships. They were going to allow him to prove that dropping out of school and taking this job at Frankie's had *not* been the worst mistake of his life but merely an unconventional method—like all the *really* rich guys took—to getting to the top faster. And in the business world everyone respected some serious hustle, right?

Todd took a deep breath and squared his shoulders, looking at the three slim envelopes in front of him. He was psyched they'd come so fast—those businesses must have really been impressed with the marketing plan for Frankie's that he'd included with his résumé. Who cared if his professor had given it a D-plus when he'd handed it in as part of a class assignment last semester? That was only because he'd focused on a small business instead of a corporation like the assignment called for. So what? He'd shown initiative *and* creativity. That was exactly the type of work real-life companies would appreciate. The old fuddy-duddy business professors at Sweet Valley U—who were only there because they couldn't get a real job anyway—were so jealous of their ingenious, aggressive students like Todd that they tried to stamp out their creativity at every turn.

It was time to put his real-world business experience and academic smarts to use.

Todd walked into the living room and flipped on his new Moby CD, propping his feet on another old pizza box while he lay on the couch and opened the first letter. How great was it going to be to run into judgmental snobs like Elizabeth and tell them about his totally selective new job? How sorry would his parents be when he showed up, briefcase in hand, for dinner and casually told them about his summer plans? And how was he going to choose between all the companies?

Dear Mr. WILKINS:
    We regret to inform you that we are unable to offer you an internship with our company this upcoming semester.

After a couple of moments of frantic ripping and tearing, the tabletop was covered with three crumpled-up balls. Todd simply stared at the mess he'd made, shaking his head in utter disbelief.
How could they all have rejected him?

Todd thought back to his applications. Had he forgotten to include a résumé? No. He'd triple checked each of the packets at Kinko's before he'd carefully put the stack in the mailbox. Everything had been spell checked, beautifully designed, printed on heavy paper. He'd even researched each of the companies on the Net so he could tailor his cover letters to them.

And what had he gotten back from each company? Form rejection letters, clearly, all without official signatures, from all three of them, none more than a paragraph long. One of the companies hadn't even spelled his last name right.

Todd shook his head, groaning. *This cannot be my life,* he thought.

The first strains of sunlight started to peek through his blinds. Todd threw up his hands to block the glare and retreated quickly to his bedroom, which became like a cave when he drew the curtains. He was becoming a total vampire, and it was *so* not cool. There had to be some mistake, some misunderstanding. Today—after he took a much needed teeny, tiny nap—he was going to call each company and clear it up. He'd slam-dunk that marketing plan right through human resources' in box.

Otherwise he'd worry that any minute now, Sarah Michelle Gellar would kick down his front door, do a triple flip through his pyramid of crushed cans, and plunge one of her trademark stakes right through his heart.

Stop eavesdropping.

Jessica Wakefield picked up a new Bic pen, stuck it in her mouth, and threw the old one on the floor, where it joined another five or six of its chewed-up little cousins.

Nice going, Jessica. Now you're going to have to pay for a whole new set of teeth in addition to a Mack truck full of Tums for this ulcer you're giving yourself.

She leaned back against her headboard, straining to pick up even the tiniest sound. Her eyes fell on the half-filled glass of water on her nightstand. Quickly she drank it, then clamped the open end of the glass against the wall and held her ear to the bottom.

Nothing.

It wasn't true, right? She was having some totally gruesome nightmare, wasn't she? Her fantastic older sister—by mere minutes, but still—wasn't up there with Sam. Was she? Late last night Jessica had heard Sam pass by her room on his way up the stairs to Elizabeth's attic room on the third floor.

She hadn't heard him go back downstairs to his own room next to the kitchen.

10

Had he spent the night upstairs with Elizabeth?

Jessica felt like she was going to hurl at the very thought. It wasn't only that Sam was the most antisocial, inconsiderate, and just plain *unfun* guy Jessica could think of. It was also that he clearly didn't like—or care about—Elizabeth. He spent half of his time picking on her and the other half of the time running away. He couldn't be counted on for anything, yet he was constantly performing all kinds of charming housemate deeds, like putting empty cartons of milk back in the fridge, paying his rent four days late and forgetting to put in the late fee, or leaving his yucky, mildew-smelling towel on the bathroom floor for *someone else* to pick up every time he took a shower.

Jessica looked at her bedside clock—6:30 A.M.—and chewed her pen even more fiercely. If she didn't get to sleep soon, she was going to be in no shape to cram for her Art History II final, which was this afternoon. Then she would have an F on top of an ulcer. *A fulcer*, she thought, and smiled grimly.

Elizabeth Wakefield with Sam Burgess, the guy who thought that washing the dishes meant rinsing a few forks and shoving the pans under the sink?

Elizabeth Wakefield with Sam Burgess, the guy

11

whose idea of a romantic date was not to dis Elizabeth for another girl *while she was in the same room?*

Elizabeth Wakefield with Sam Burgess, whose middle name was Can't and whose last name was Commit?

Jessica picked up her art book to study, took the pen out of her mouth, then gave up and threw them both against the far wall. "Argh!" she screamed into her pillow.

Jessica, they stopped taking nominations for Best Sister in a House of Freaks last week at the Academy, don't you remember? she could almost hear her best friend and final housemate, Neil Martin, gently reminding her.

Sighing, she got up and shuffled over to the far side of her room to pick up her book. It was open to a very famous picture by the Dutch painter Van Eyck. They had spent weeks on it in class: a pinched, ferretlike nobleman with his pregnant wife, both facing the viewer unsmiling in their sixteenth-century Flemish duds. The woman, Jessica's professor had informed them, wasn't really pregnant. The couple was having trouble having children, so the husband had told Van Eyck to paint her that way for luck. It was a totally creepy picture, and looking at it for too long always gave Jessica the shivers. She picked up the book, holding it at arm's length while she looked into the couple's eyes, as if at any moment they were going to jump out of the picture and into her room.

Ferret face, stockings, and all, she would still rather stuff Sam Burgess under the sink and set her sister up on a blind date with *this* guy than see her fall for Sam and suffer all over again, any day of the week.

Finally some well-deserved silence in the House of Pain.

Neil Martin lay curled in the fetal position, a makeshift tent of pillows placed strategically around him. He was wearing a satin United Airlines eye mask and heavy-duty, rock-star-style earplugs, and he had hiked his quilt over his head to prevent any further light from disturbing his hard-won slumber.

"Aaahh," Neil breathed, insinuating himself even deeper into his burrow.

Thump. Something hit the wall right about his headboard, it seemed, at light speed and roused Neil as if it had been a marching band. Neil lurched straight up in bed like a zombie.

"What *now?*" He groaned.

For the past week, every morning Neil had woken up feeling like he'd just completed a grueling triathlon instead of having slept for the eight hours he rigorously insisted on every night. Finally, under the piercing, pins-and-needles staccato of a hot shower, Neil had realized the problem. Every muscle of his body, from his eyelids to his toes, was pulled as tight as a banjo string.

His housemates, Neil realized, were creating an atmosphere as unhealthy for him as if they were happily puffing away on Camel Lights two feet from him twenty-four hours a day. Sam burst in and out of the house at all hours, stopping only long enough to do something that would trip wire Jessica, like leaving a peanut-butter sandwich in a crack of the couch, or throw Elizabeth into a tailspin, like getting into one of his now famous fights with her. Living with Elizabeth lately reminded Neil of two hellish weeks he had once spent in the company of his teenage cousin, Gloria: all tragic death masks, fits of weeping, and sullen silence. It'd been clear to Neil for weeks that Sam and Elizabeth were crazy about each other, but they seemed to prefer bringing out the worst sides of each other to intertwining flutes of champagne at Yum-Yums.

It was all too much for Neil. Neil was a Virgo, and there were two nonnegotiables in his sign: stability and quiet. Sam and Elizabeth had shredded the first, and Jessica was having a furious go with a pair of scissors at the latter.

Ah, Jessica. He loved the girl like a madman, and they'd been drawn together as friends out of a similar sense of glamour and scene stealing. But didn't the girl understand about private time? Space? A little R and R to go with the gossip and griping? Jessica was like a flight attendant on a plane on which Neil was the only passenger, except instead of interrupting him with blankets and vacuum-sealed peanuts, she unleashed monologues like Meryl Streep.

He truly loved all of his roommates, actually. But lately he felt like he was locked in a cell that showed reruns of *Days of Our Lives* twenty-four hours a day. At this rate Neil was either going to go prematurely gray or flat-out crazy before junior year: not the best way to find a snackable boyfriend or kick off a political career.

There was no more avoiding the facts of the situation. For Neil to achieve any measure of personal happiness—and stop suffering from sleep deprivation—one of two things was going to have to happen: Either his roommates had to be put in suspended animation à la Sigourney Weaver in *Alien 3,* or he was going to have to move out.

Instead of terrifying him, the thought of moving out filled Neil with the first sense of relief he'd experienced in weeks.

Jessica was his best friend, but they would both benefit from a teensy separation. And he *knew* her. She would be really upset at first, but she would also understand.

And he would get over whatever guilt was currently creeping into his thoughts. Sad but finally at ease, Neil lay back and fell into the first real sleep he'd gotten in two weeks.

Chapter Two

Sam Burgess yawned and opened his eyes. A pink curtain and a row of journalism books swam into his view. Down near his legs, he saw what looked very much like the sneakers of . . . Elizabeth Wakefield. He bolted upright. Wait—where was he?

He had been having a very pleasant dream, it seemed, in which he was no longer fighting with Elizabeth. They had kissed, even. For Sam it had felt like a pure surge of adrenaline and joy through his entire body.

Clearly it hadn't been a dream.

He rubbed his head, looking down at the sleeping Elizabeth. Her blond hair covered half her face. Before he could stop himself, he reached over and tucked the loose strands behind her ear.

Don't freak out, he told himself.

Sam didn't know whether his proximity to the

girl who had obsessed him for all of the past year made him want to bury himself in her arms forever or run screaming into the quad. Last night they had finally talked honestly—well, they'd talked a little. They must have fallen asleep in each other's arms. Would Elizabeth think they were going out now? Was that what *he* wanted?

Sam felt a leaden brick descend into his gut, and his stomach twisted painfully. The walls in Elizabeth's bedroom suddenly seemed to become very, very close.

Whoa, calm down, man, Sam told himself. *This is Elizabeth, the girl you've been waiting for this whole year. She's your friend—not a school of piranhas.*

Elizabeth groaned and began to stretch out. She opened her eyes and pressed her face directly into Sam's T-shirt. "Mmmff," she said.

Now, listen up, Sam. Remember—this is the girl you want. The cold war between you two the past two months has been hell. Don't mess this up.

Sam swallowed deeply and tried to smile. "Hey, sleepyhead," he said, trying to ignore the fact that he felt like his sneakers had suddenly been specially outfitted with booster rockets.

"Hello, yourself," Elizabeth said. She buried her head in his T-shirt again and looked up, giving him a shy smile. "Fancy meeting you here."

Sam returned her smile and told himself to put his arm around her. For a moment they shifted awkwardly around on the bed. "Yeah, uh, I've been looking into properties in this region," he joked.

Elizabeth raised an eyebrow. "What do you think of the place?" she asked, propping herself up on her elbow.

Sam swallowed again and tried to calm his breathing. Elizabeth's eyes were so *clear,* he noticed each time he looked into them, and so blue. "It's not half bad," he said. Slowly their faces leaned toward each other's, and they kissed—a gentle, quiet kiss that sent a jolt through Sam's entire body.

Elizabeth's too, as far as his arm could tell. She was trembling all over.

They pulled apart and looked into each other's eyes. Sam took in a couple of short, shallow breaths. "Well, I try," Elizabeth finally said.

Sam tried to think of a funny answer but found that his head felt like it had been scooped out like the inside of a pumpkin on Halloween. It was a pretty uncomfortable feeling, and he concentrated on looking at the space between Elizabeth's eyes instead of into them—a technique he had developed when he couldn't look his father in the eye during fights—to make it go away.

Elizabeth gave him a shy kiss on the cheek, then

snuggled down and pressed her face into his neck. "It's still early," she purred. "I could sleep for the rest of the day, we were up so late last night."

Sam felt like her words were a huge hammer, splattering his pumpkin head with a tremendous *whomp*. Wait—did Elizabeth expect him to spend all day in bed with her? What *did* she expect? After his constant bickering with his family, he had had enough of people telling him where to go, what to do, and how he could do it. Why was everyone always trying to box him in? From now on, would Elizabeth expect them to be joined at the hip until graduation?

He looked down at Elizabeth's head. She had dropped down onto his chest and was already snoring lightly. Her arm was thrown across his stomach so that her hand curled around his waist. He could feel their two chests rise and fall together with every breath.

Evidently she did.

Chloe Murphy plucked a strand of auburn hair out of her eyes, trying to make sure it wasn't flipping back at each side, à la the 1970s, like it had been doing lately. The wind blew it right back. She looked at herself in the reflection of the library's windows as she walked by on her way to the cafeteria. Trying not to be too obvious, she ticked off all of her faults: boring hair, boring face, boring clothes. Boring life. It was hopeless.

Finals were descending like a lead balloon, her freshman year was almost finished, and she had yet to snag a boyfriend. She'd thought that after she pledged Theta Alpha Theta, she could snag a guy as easily as picking up a carton of milk at the dining hall. Unfortunately for Chloe, finding a boyfriend at SVU was more like searching for a Quarter Pounder at Burger King. That was, of course, if you didn't count Martin—who, frankly, had seemed much, much too eager to run off with Chloe's friend Val for someone who was supposedly obsessed with a certain other someone. It was like freshman year was some huge game of musical chairs, and every time she tried to play, Chloe was the one left standing.

When she'd first come to Sweet Valley, she'd tried as hard as possible not to fall in with the dorky crowd she'd been stuck with in high school. And she'd done okay, it was true. She had cool upperclassman friends like Jessica and, she was still hard-pressed to believe, Nina Harper. Plus Chloe was in Theta, definitely the "it" sorority on campus. And she tried to make herself as social as possible, eschewing the library and dorm for hangouts like frat parties, campus events, and Yum-Yums, the cool campus coffee bar.

Still, she might as well have been wearing a Post-it that said Ignore Me on her forehead for all the good her efforts had done. For instance, last night she had gone out with Nina to SVU's annual Hot Dog Festival. Not only was Nina pretty and fun, but she was never at a loss for boyfriends. With her smooth brown skin, almond-shaped eyes, shoulder-length curly hair, and sexy clothes, guys were constantly checking her out. So while she and Nina had trolled the aisles at the festival, Chloe had thought that some of the male attention would have to shift over to her, even by accident.

Not even. The guys had looked at Nina appreciatively, then turned to the next alluring item: the rows of glistening hot dogs.

Chloe pushed open the doors to the cafeteria and doubled back, her attention caught by the sign for the SVU Spring Semiformal. It was a huge blowup of Leonardo DiCaprio's face, with the words *Get on Board* coming in a balloon out of his mouth. Leo wasn't Chloe's type, but the sight of his grinning, moony face, the face that was speaking to hundreds of girls with boyfriends and dates—or at least wanna-be dates—made her feel like she'd achieved a new level of loserdom since her days of rubber bands and braces.

Chloe sighed and joined the huge mass that fed into the hot-foods line. She was surrounded by chatting couples, groups of friends, and teams that had just finished their morning workouts, sucking back on water bottles while they fanned their sweaty T-shirts. Only she—friendless Chloe—was alone.

Chloe picked up an orange plastic tray and grabbed a chocolate milk and some napkins. Wait—there was definitely another lone girl in the line. Two people in front of her, a tall brunette—clearly an upperclassman—placed a bowl of oatmeal next to a grapefruit juice.

Chloe squared her shoulders and stood up a little straighter. Well, that girl was alone, wasn't she? And she was very pretty, with tan, smooth legs and a profile like Jennifer Lopez's. The brunette was an independent, strong woman, and so was Chloe.

Suddenly one of the athletes in front of Chloe jostled ahead and began to speak to the girl in low tones. Chloe strained to hear. Maybe he was just asking about biology homework or something.

"So, uh . . . ," Chloe heard the guy say as she held her cup under the coffee machine a little longer than necessary, "you wanna go?"

The girl turned back to the jock and flashed him a huge smile. She was as pretty as Jennifer Lopez from the front too. "I'd love to go," Chloe heard her say. "I've actually never gone to one of the dances here before."

"Oh, yeah?" said the guy. "I can't believe that."

"Well, swimming keeps me really busy," the girl began. The couple kept chatting and headed off toward one of the tables.

"Hey," said the guy behind the counter. "Hey, you."

Chloe snapped back to reality and looked at the steaming heaps of eggs, French toast, and oatmeal in front of her. "Are you eating breakfast, or did you just stop by to meditate?"

The students around Chloe broke into laughter. Chloe flushed deeply. "Just give me some of everything," she said. Weaving through the loud crowd, Chloe grabbed some more napkins and headed to an empty table in the corner. She dabbed at the corner of her eyes lightly with a napkin. She was not going to burst into tears in front of the entire school—she was not. Searching for something else to concentrate on, she looked down at her own tray. Yuck. Cheddar-cheese omelette, bacon, hash browns—what had she been thinking? Her weight—that must be the problem. All of that snacking during rush had added on the famous freshman fifteen. Well, freshman five, maybe. Chloe was as slim as she'd always been.

Still, feeling better, she pushed away her tray and took a demure sip of her chocolate milk. Only healthy, wholesome foods from now on, like that

Jennifer Lopez clone. When she was slinkier looking, the guys would come flocking.

They'd *better*.

Is he still sleeping or what?

For the umpteenth time, it seemed, Elizabeth sneaked a glance in Sam's direction. His eyes were definitely closed, but so was his mouth, and he was holding his legs and arms much too stiffly—like a little woodland animal frozen in the gaze of a wily predator.

"Hey," she said, poking him in the stomach. "Want to get going?"

Sam opened his eyes. Clearly he hadn't been sleeping at all, merely playing possum. "I was just waiting for you," he said.

Elizabeth waited uncomfortably for a moment. What was that supposed to mean? Since when had she become the boss of the world?

"Well, I'm starving," she finally said, introducing a note of heartiness to her tone to try to set Sam at ease. Something in his tone told her that he probably wasn't going to want to slumber around and kiss her all morning, like she'd hoped.

Sam immediately jumped up like she'd said there was an anaconda in the bed. "Great!" he said, much too enthusiastically. "Why don't I take us both to breakfast at Yum-Yums?"

Much better, Elizabeth thought. He must just

be really nervous. "I'd love that," she said, standing across the room so that it didn't seem like she was trying to get Sam to come back into bed with her. "I'll just jump in the shower."

Sam raised his eyebrows and exhaled, like Elizabeth had just told him she was going to have to go in for a four-hour facial. Then he immediately wiped that look off his face and replaced it with a stiff, seemingly honest look of polite interest. "Okay," he said. "I'll be downstairs."

Elizabeth felt like Sam was trying to sidle around her politely to get to the door—like *she* had become the anaconda. "Aren't you forgetting something?" she said, then instantly regretted it.

Sam's eyes blazed like she had zapped him with an angry stick. "You bet," he said coolly, and leaned over and kissed her stiffly on the cheek.

Oh, jeez, Elizabeth, she berated herself. *Remember to cool it with the cutesy sorority-girl act around Mr. Jumpy, will you?*

Sam had opened the door already and was about to bolt. Elizabeth grabbed his hand.

"Sam," she said, striving to make herself sound calm and not all needy. "It'll be great to go to breakfast. We'll really have a chance to talk about last night and . . . everything."

Sam's eyes changed again, but this time they became little dry stones. "Sure," he said flatly, and disengaged himself. "See you downstairs."

Elizabeth kicked herself inwardly, then immediately felt like kicking Sam. Why was he so goddamn mercurial? Would it kill him to just sit down with her and relax over a bagel for an hour or two?

I'm not contagious, Elizabeth thought angrily, then immediately giggled, picturing Sam suddenly becoming as earnest and up front as she was. *But maybe I should be.*

She grabbed her robe and flip-flops and headed over to the bathroom. As she turned on the water and the bathroom began to fill with steam, she started picturing what it might be like to really be able to *talk* with Sam—to have him not just as a boyfriend, but as a friend and partner. Elizabeth knew her friends were going to say she was crazy, but she didn't want the kind of guy who showed up at her door with a handful of gladiolas and a stretch limo. Finn Robinson, the med student she'd dated, had been that kind of guy, hadn't he? And look how much his supposed "romantic" side had said about him!

Sam might be a complicated guy, but at least he wasn't a liar—not to himself and not to others. And if he decided to do something, you knew it would be real. If he dated Elizabeth, he would be doing it for the right reasons, not because he was bored, because other people would think it was cool, or because he liked to rack up girls like poker chips.

27

He's not Finn, Elizabeth thought. *And he's not like me either. He's himself.*

She didn't want a clone of herself. She wanted Sam just as he was—moody, distant, difficult. But she also wanted a Sam who knew that Elizabeth was on his side and that he didn't have to be scared of her. A Sam who was able to be on Elizabeth's side too.

Elizabeth began to lather her hair with Jessica's special banana shampoo, an incredibly expensive blend that Jessica ordered especially from Australia. Well, Jessica borrowed her stuff all the time. She'd live.

God, what was her sister going to say?

Elizabeth began to lather her hair more fiercely, unconsciously tensing for the fight she knew she was going to have to have very soon with Jessica.

"It's my decision and no one else's," Elizabeth said aloud to the tiled walls. That made her feel better. *And Sam's too,* she quickly added. Oops.

Well, whatever happened, getting a grip on this thing with Sam would certainly be a very, very interesting way to spend the summer.

The ad had read, *Single room available in two-bedroom apartment. Sunny, quiet,* and Neil fervently hoped that the last was true. On the phone

28

the girl had sounded nice and calm, but how much could you tell from a phone call? For all he knew, Elizabeth might sound like a yoga instructor when she answered their phone at home, and look at the way *she'd* been acting lately.

Neil turned the corner onto the street listed in the ad and started checking the house numbers. About two houses in, he saw it. Bordered by green, leafy oaks, with a large wraparound porch and shuttered windows, the house did look very restful, almost like a country inn. But would the girl he'd spoken to turn out to be Norman Bates in an old gray wig?

Neil took a big breath and mounted the steps. He stuck the ripped-out ad in his pocket and rapped quickly on the front door.

Almost immediately the door opened. A friendly-looking girl in jeans with long, straight hair and bare feet stuck out her hand. "Hi, I'm Mona," she said, smiling. "You must be Neil."

Relieved, Neil shook her hand heartily and smiled back. "Guilty as charged," he said.

Mona laughed. "C'mon upstairs," she said. "Kathy's room is a little messy from all the boxes, but you'll be able to get the general idea."

Neil followed Mona up the polished oak stairway to a clean landing with a small Doisneau print on the wall. "Mrs. Cheatham lives downstairs," Mona said in an exaggerated whisper, pointing downward. "This is her place. She's totally nice; she's just kind of old. So we have to keep pretty quiet."

Neil had been worried she was going to say Mrs. Cheatham had five kids, all under the age of ten. "That's no problem," he said. "My partying days are over."

"I know what you mean," Mona said, opening the door into a tidy, sunny living room with a row of plants on the windowsill. "It gets pretty old after a while, doesn't it?"

"Old enough to leave home and get a job," Neil responded, looking with interest at the books on the mantel.

Mona laughed again. "You're really funny," she said. "Let me show you the place."

Mona walked Neil through a narrow hallway, pointing out a shining, black-and-white-tiled kitchen—with all the original forties fixtures still intact, he noted. "Cool, huh?" Mona said.

Together they walked into a large, airy back bedroom. "Mine's on the other side of the kitchen, and the bathroom's in the middle," Mona explained. "Kathy and I are big believers in privacy."

Neil was already starting to picture where he would put his bed. His desk would go by the window, and his Klimt poster would look incredible on the far wall. . . .

"So," said Mona, turning to him. "D'ya like it?"

Neil turned to her, barely able to contain his glee. "Can I give you a check right now?" he asked.

"Can you ever," said Mona. "I'm so psyched not to have to let a million strangers through here."

Walking back out onto the sunny street, Neil felt like a huge load had been lifted from his shoulders. But wait—should he have told Mona he was gay? Neil slowed down for a second and considered going back. Then he remembered the books on the shelf and relaxed: It wasn't likely that someone with a copy of Dan Savage's *The Kid* and Gertrude Stein's *The Autobiography of Alice B. Toklas* was going to have any problem with him.

Wondering how Mona might react to the fact that he was gay made him think about the problems he'd had with one of his current roomies, Jessica—namely, fighting over the same guys.

Neil pictured Mona's tidy apartment: cat posters; all of Joni Mitchell's albums; huge stacks of books in her bedroom, almost threatening to topple over on her very simple futon.

Somehow he didn't think that overlapping swains and social schedules were going to be a huge problem with the barefooted Mona.

Chapter Three

After Chloe finished breakfast, she went back home, to the Theta Alpha Theta sorority house, to try to study. The first-floor lounge was filled with Thetas, all bent over books, many chewing gum, pencils, or the ends of their ponytails. Chloe paged through her Intro to Psychology textbook and tried to concentrate like her sorority sisters, but she was too distracted by her unhappiness. She felt like everyone had been given some secret password to a social life except her. What did they know that she didn't? And what did they have that she was missing?

Nina! Nina would be able to help her. Chloe closed her book with a bang and stood up, reinvigorated. She stuffed some pencils and notebooks in a bag and headed off across campus, chewing her own hair in excitement.

Just that year Nina had transformed herself from a shy bookworm into the attractive bombshell Chloe was now in awe of. Nina had had problems dating before . . . hadn't she? She would not only be able to understand Chloe's position, but she could give Chloe advice—and some wardrobe tips.

Chloe vaulted up the steps to Nina's dorm room and knocked excitedly on the door. Thank heavens she was home—Chloe could hear paper rustling and footsteps in the background. Hopefully Nina would be able to tear herself away from her books long enough to give Chloe the fashion boost she needed.

Nina opened the door in her trademark studying uniform: an old sweatshirt and jeans. "Hey, Chloe," she said. "What's up?"

Chloe clapped and made an excited face. "Nina," she said. "I need your help."

Nina clapped too and made a mock-excited face back. "What with?" she said.

Chloe walked in and dropped her bag by Nina's desk. She grimaced at her reflection in the mirror over Nina's bureau. "I need a new look," she said.

Nina unsuccessfully tried to hold back a laugh and walked over to her desk and sat down. "What for?" she asked.

Chloe jiggled one foot against the other, stroking some of the cardigans tossed over the back of Nina's bed frame. "Well, first of all, for the semiformal," she said.

Nina snorted. "Oh," she said. "Well, that shouldn't be too big of a problem. I think I have my Heidi Klum cloning unit under the bed."

Chloe rolled her eyes and sighed. "I *wish*," she said.

Nina shot Chloe a look of surprise. "Chloe," she said. "I was just kidding. You're great just the way you are. Don't you know that?"

Chloe was fluffing her hair in the mirror, wondering if her bangs made her look too young. She turned to Nina in exasperation. "That's easy for you to say," she said. She was surprised to realize that tears were welling up in her eyes. She swallowed them back down as quickly as she could. "Everyone *looks* at you."

Nina walked over and sat next to Chloe. She looked at her very seriously. "Listen, Chloe, if you dressed sexy, guys would look at you too," she began.

"I know," Chloe interrupted. "That's why I need your closet. For inspiration."

"Let me finish," Nina said. "Chloe: If you dress sexy, guys will look at you too. But they're not looking at *you*. They're looking at the clothes

34

and what they think the clothes mean."

"They mean that you're sexy," said Chloe excitedly.

"Girl, act like you have some sense." Nina laughed. "They mean—or at least boys think they mean—that you're gonna have sex with them."

Chloe had stopped listening already. She was examining a short dress with a gray metallic overlay. "Do you think this is still in the stores?" she said.

"Listen," Nina said. "It's not like there's anything wrong with dressing sexy. I like to look sexy sometimes. But I'm not doing it to get guys. I'm doing it for myself."

Chloe was holding up a pair of black boot-cut pants against herself and examining the style in the mirror. "Uh-huh," she said.

"Guys that are interested in you because you're dressing sexy are only interested in the sex part of things," Nina continued. "The minute they get you, they dump you."

Chloe was thinking that Nina had probably gotten dumped because she was too uptight. And lectury. But she merely shrugged, then looked with longing at Nina's red pony-hair boots.

"There's a difference," Nina finished, "between *fashion* and *foolishness*."

And there's a difference, Chloe thought, *between* fun *and* fuddy-duddy.

Nina yawned and opened up her book again. "Personally, I'm not sleeping with any guy again until I hear the *l* word."

Chloe had moved on to Nina's jewelry box. She fingered a pink beaded choker. "Can I borrow this for the dance?" she asked.

Nina looked at Chloe, bemused. "Chloe, have you even started studying for your finals yet?" she said.

Chloe tried to look truthful. "Of course!" she said, gesturing at her bag.

Nina leaned over and looked inside, then raised her eyebrows. She wagged her finger in Chloe's direction. "If you don't watch out, Chloe," she warned, "you're going to be attending the semi-formal with your Shop-rite name tag."

Neil cracked open the door to the house, feeling a little like he was trespassing in his own home. Inside, it was as quiet as Mona's apartment. *Of course, now the place gets calm, the minute I get a new place,* Neil thought. He looked around the perfectly clean kitchen and jumped back when he opened the fridge. Rows of juice, eggs in their plastic indentations, and gleaming racks with vegetables, cold cuts, yogurts, and cheese slices stared back at him. All of the hockey-puck salami slices, takeout containers, and unknown foil-wrapped lumps from weeks ago had been thrown out, evidently. What was going on? Had some alien cleaning force invaded the house? And where *was* everybody?

Neil poured himself a glass of orange juice and peeked through the swinging door. He walked toward the living room, which also looked ferociously tidy. Neil didn't know whether to clap with joy or get wildly suspicious. *No* one ever cleaned up the place except him or Elizabeth, and of late, Elizabeth had been too busy fighting with Sam to do any more than wash the occasional dish. Someone must have caught the housecleaning bug around here.

Running his finger along the top of the stereo system (dust-free!), he almost bypassed Jessica lying on the living-room couch, staring into her art-history textbook as if her life depended on it.

Looking at his best friend, so serious and quiet, Neil hoped that Jessica wouldn't have too hard a time with the news. Not only did he not want to hurt her feelings, he really didn't want to be the cause of a big, dramatic scene. "Hey," he said, grabbing a coaster and placing his juice glass on the shined-to-a-mirror-glare coffee table.

Jessica looked up briefly, then back down at her book. "Hey," she said dully.

For a second Neil had the crazy thought that Jessica knew exactly where he'd been and had been home stewing ever since she'd found out.

Almost as quickly he dismissed it. It's not like there wasn't enough drama in this house to go around. "What's up?" he said. "Do you know anything about the cleaning fairy who made a visit to our humble abode?"

Jessica smiled slightly, then looked back down again. "I was having a little obsessional fit," she said.

"Well," Neil cracked, "better over the house than a guy."

"Let's hope we can say the same for my sister," Jessica said.

Normally Neil would have been lured in by a cryptic statement like that, but he was putting his foot down. After all, half his problem was caused by him indicating that he wasn't averse to letting everyone unload their problems on him, seven days a week, twenty-four hours a day.

Jessica sighed hugely, waiting for a response. Neil only grinned back at her. This passive-aggressive stuff could be kind of fun when you weren't on the receiving end of it.

"Listen, Jess," he finally said, but she wasn't looking at him. She had turned her head to the stairs, where a barrage of footsteps could be heard. Neil followed her gaze.

Sam Burgess came down the steps, nodded at them both, and then walked down the hall to his room. He closed the door behind him.

Neil looked at Jessica, and Jessica looked at Neil. She slowly closed her eyes, then opened them again. "Oh. My. God," she finally said. "So I was right. He *did* go up there last night. And he's just coming down now. What happened to Elizabeth's taste in guys?"

Neil immediately went into red-alert mode. "Now, Jessica, calm down," he began.

It was too late. Jessica had already abandoned her art book and was racing up the steps two at a time. Neil heard frantic knocking, then a door slamming and a clamor of voices.

Neil exhaled and sat down heavily on the couch. Upstairs, the voices grew louder and louder. Neil began to breathe forcefully and deeply, meditating on the orange-juice glass so he didn't feel that he had to run upstairs immediately and play referee.

"Are you kidding me, Liz!" he heard faintly through the ceiling.

He had clearly escaped just in the nick of time.

Jessica felt like she had been sent to an alternate universe as she stood in Elizabeth's steamy bathroom, having to shout over the drone of the shower spray.

This day was getting weirder and weirder, and it wasn't even nine o'clock! First she had weirdly been stricken with the cleaning bug, even though she was usually comforted, not stressed out, by the general chaos of the house: heaps of unwashed laundry and a fridge crammed so full with leftovers, it was hard to close. She had scrubbed the kitchen floor so hard, she had ruined the French manicure she had splurged on only last week—*a twenty-five-dollar* investment.

Next Neil had disappeared early this morning—just when she needed to talk to him most—and, when he finally showed up, acted like some robot Neil, not the best friend she was used to gossiping and having endless heart-to-hearts with.

Then the kicker—Sam coming down the stairs instead of emerging from his own pit of a room by the kitchen.

How could Elizabeth get involved with that commitmentphobic, lying slacker? Sam wasn't one of those guys who was a jerk in disguise—he was totally open about his jerk ways and unapologetic! Yeah, Sam was really good-looking and had his deep moments. And yeah, he and Elizabeth had a long history. But after the stuff he'd pulled on Elizabeth two months ago? How could she?

Elizabeth finally emerged from the shower, a towel around her. "Jessica," she said, rubbing baby oil onto her smooth legs, "I'm not going to defend Sam right now. I know this seems really sudden. Especially after the past couple of months. But trust me, okay? I know what I'm doing."

Jessica wanted to take the bottle of baby oil and douse it all over Elizabeth's head. "So you *are* getting involved with Sam?"

Jessica would have preferred a teeth cleaning to the sparkle that appeared in Elizabeth's eyes the minute she said Sam's name.

"We are talking about Sam Burgess, right?" Jessica asked. "That guy always walking around here with the sullen, moody expression?"

Elizabeth started rubbing her hair with a towel. "Jessica, don't start."

Jessica began to practically stutter. "You're the one who shouldn't start," she said, picking up the brush Elizabeth was gesturing at with one hand. She held the brush back for a second. "Elizabeth," she said, her voice becoming serious. "Did you sleep with him?"

Elizabeth took the brush, a dreamy expression crossing her face. "No. Not . . . yet."

Jessica honestly thought she was going to hurl. The bathroom didn't have room to pace, so she picked up a conditioner bottle to shake in her sister's direction. "Elizabeth! You *cannot* sleep with him."

Elizabeth held up a bottle of mascara. "Is this black going to look too dark on me?"

Jessica snatched the bottle of Maybelline away

41

and threw it on the counter. "Elizabeth, can we put a stop to makeover madness for just a second?" Elizabeth picked up the bottle, calm as could be, and started applying a little mascara on her top lashes. "You cannot be serious about this thing with Sam."

Elizabeth sighed. "Jess, I appreciate that you're concerned. I really do. But I *am* serious." She looked directly at Jessica, and for a second Elizabeth was once again the smart, serious twin. "I'm *crazy* about Sam. You know how I feel about him."

"Elizabeth!" Jessica screamed. "He is a lying, cheating slacker!"

Elizabeth capped the bottle of mascara and threw it down on the counter, then planted her hands on her hips. "Look, Jessica, I know Sam's got a lot of explaining to do. But I also know he's a great guy. And anyway, you and I have been through this."

Jessica couldn't keep her voice down anymore. "That's great, Elizabeth! Just great! Now you're *defending* him to me."

"Well, I wouldn't have to defend him if you didn't attack him," Elizabeth said. "You think I don't know every single one of Sam's worst traits? Jessica, I lived through them *personally*."

Jessica clenched her fists to her sides. "So how can you trust him after what he's done to you— *twice*?"

"I can't argue about this now," Elizabeth said. "I have to get dressed—we're going to breakfast."

"Elizabeth, please listen to me." Jessica plucked the blush brush from Elizabeth's hands. "He is going to *totally* screw you over."

Elizabeth snatched the brush back. "You know what, Jess? Maybe he will. And maybe he won't. All I know is that I'm willing to see this through, wherever it might lead. I really want it to work. And anyway, I'm the one who needs to forgive the stuff he pulled on me—not you. So just be happy for me that Sam and I have finally hooked up after the crazy year we've had, okay?"

Jessica sat down on the edge of the bathtub. "No." She looked Elizabeth in the eye through the mirror. "I can't."

Elizabeth met her gaze. "Well, I'm really sorry to hear that. Gotta get dressed, Jessica." She put her towel back on the hook, then headed down the hall to her bedroom.

Jessica stood in the doorway of the bathroom, feeling like she was watching Neve Campbell go back into the house during *Scream* or something. "Elizabeth, stop!" she yelled desperately. "That mascara is *way* too black!"

Chloe left Nina's dorm, feeling that she'd definitely gotten some usable concepts from Miss

Where's-my-textbook-and-glasses. Tight, boot-cut jeans . . . beaded chokers . . . tiny tank top. . . . It was going to come together; she could feel it. Thank God, Nina hadn't given away all her sexy items when she'd decided that dressing with abandon was no longer the key to happiness.

Chloe decided to stop by and see if her friend Val Berger wanted to go shopping too. On the way over to Oakley Hall she stopped by the student-center cafeteria to pick up one of those snack bags of baby carrots, even though she was dying for a slice of pizza with ricotta and spinach. That chocolate milk wasn't as filling as she'd thought it was going to be, but she was determined not to break her diet.

Since Val had started dating Martin, Chloe's sort-of ex-boyfriend, things had been slightly tense between her and Chloe. Chloe, however, was doing her best to act like she couldn't care less that the guy who'd been crushing on her was now happily paired off with the—Chloe felt she had to admit—considerably less pretty Val. Because how embarrassing would it be to seem jealous of Val— over *Martin*?

Chloe reached Oakley and took the stairs up to the third floor. Val's dorm-room door was open, so Chloe gave a tap and walked in to find Val and her roommate, Deena, sitting at their desks, their noses pressed in textbooks. Chloe flopped down on Deena's bed, ripping open the bag of carrots and chomping down on the nubbins as quickly as she could. "Hello? You guys are, like, totally zoned out on studying!"

"Oh, hey, Chlo," Val said, not even lifting her bent head.

"So do you want to come to the mall?" Chloe asked. "'Cause I'm going to pick up some new duds." For Val, Chloe dropped the I-need-a-new-look speech. The only people in Val and Deena's room who needed a new look, in Chloe's opinion, were Val and Deena, both of whom seemed to think that turtlenecks and corduroys were perfect for the sunny skies, moderate temperatures, and trendiness of Sweet Valley.

"Oh, I can't." Val groaned. "I'd love to—I have to get a dress for the dance, but I've got so much studying to do."

Chloe looked at Val suspiciously. Was Val trying to give Chloe a little dig about the dance? *And* about finals? Did even her dorky friends know how pathetic she was?

Deena glanced up from her book. She eyed Chloe's carrot sticks. "I hope that's not your lunch," she said. "And I hope you're not getting any on my bed. I just washed that comforter."

"Don't worry," Chloe said. "And carrots make

a great lunch. It's good to cleanse out your body of toxins occasionally."

Deena rolled her eyes. "Cleanse, shmens," she said, crossing one thickish leg over the other. Deena wasn't fat, exactly, but still—Chloe would *die* if she looked like her, so solid and unshakable. "I'm so sick of skinny girls who diet."

Secretly Chloe felt a triumphant flush that Deena had called her skinny, but she tried not to show it. "Yeah, well—sometimes I just lose my appetite."

Val laughed. "You didn't look like you had lost your appetite at the Hot Dog Festival," she said.

Chloe flushed again, this time from embarrassment. Last night she had easily crammed a good four or five hot dogs into her mouth in the first half hour, but she hadn't thought anyone noticed. Was that why boys weren't talking to her—because they thought she was a greedy pig? God, there were pitfalls everywhere.

Chloe sat up and crumpled the now empty bag of carrots. "I was really hungry—I hadn't eaten anything yet that day," she said defensively. "Anyway, I was only trying to keep up with Nina."

"Don't be so sensitive." Deena laughed. "Val and I just don't want you to diet so much, you make *us* lose *our* appetites."

That might not be such a bad thing, Chloe almost responded nastily. She stopped herself just in time. Huh. Some support network for her self-improvement program her friends were turning out to be.

"Well, I better go," Chloe said, standing up. She turned to Deena. "*You* don't feel like going shopping for a dress, do you?"

Deena looked back at Chloe with laughter in her eyes, as if she knew exactly what the subtext of Chloe's question was. "No," she responded merrily. "I don't know what color to get yet—I'm still choosing amongst my many swains."

Chloe closed the door behind her, her cheeks burning. She would *die*—absolutely *die*—if Deena got a date for the dance and she didn't.

She *had* been joking with that "many swains" comment, hadn't she?

Chapter Four

Todd lay on his unmade bed amid his pile of cover letters and copies of his marketing report. Before he took a nap, he was going to go through these companies—thoroughly—and call them to find out what was going on.

Todd called the first company, SPF Worldgroup, Inc. SPF, he had learned from the Web site, had sites in Geneva, London, Paris, and Bangkok. Todd could just picture himself settling down into first class on the Concorde and unscrewing one of those minibottles of Drambuie, then clinking glasses with the gorgeous woman next to him. "Oh, me?" he would say humbly. "I'm in finance. . . ."

Todd shook himself out of his reverie—how long had he been on hold already, two weeks? The Kenny G sound track wasn't helping either.

Finally a human voice clicked in. "SPF Worldgroup," it said impatiently.

Todd hastened to sound brusque and professional too. "Thanks very much, good morning to you," he put in quickly. "I'm calling for . . . uh . . . Georgia English," he finished lamely, finally finding the name of the human-resources director at the top of the page.

"Ms. English is on another call right now. Can I take a message?" the voice said, sounding like it was dying to click down the receiver and get back to work. Todd panicked.

"No, um . . . I mean, I'm responding to her letter, and I just thought . . . um, can I hold for her?" Todd finally finished.

"Ms. English sent you a letter?" the voice asked.

Todd hesitated. Well, a rejection letter was still a letter, wasn't it? He forged ahead. "Yes," he said.

The voice sounded infinitely more pleasant. "May I ask what it was in regard to?" the voice inquired.

"The marketing internship," Todd responded confidently. This was going better every second.

"Ah, yes, she's been expecting your call," the voice said warmly. "I'll put you through."

Todd almost dropped the receiver as if it was on fire. They'd been expecting him to call! They knew there had been a mistake too, and they wanted to correct it. But wait—how could they? Had he even told the receptionist his name? Well, a big company like that must have caller ID.

After three short buzzes a woman picked up the line. "Georgia English," she said crisply.

"Hi, this is Todd Wilkins."

The woman's voice immediately sounded nonplussed. "I don't understand," Ms. English said. "I thought this was a call from the candidate for the marketing internship."

"Um, it is . . . sort of," Todd said. "I applied for the marketing internship, and I think there's been a mistake."

Ms. English sounded infinitely less friendly each second. "What kind of mistake? What are you talking about?" she asked.

This woman certainly had no idea who he was. "Well, I got rejected," Todd said.

Ms. English was silent for a moment. "Mr. Wilkins," she said finally, "are you aware of how many applications we receive for this position every year?"

Don't let her brush you off, Todd thought. His smooth, cool salesman side—the one he used to resolve disputes at the bar—kicked in. "Ms. English, of course I'm aware of how competitive the position is. That's why I'm calling. I'm an extremely competitive candidate, and I think SPF must have made a mistake in knocking me out of the rounds so quickly."

Silence.

Todd gathered his last bit of courage and pushed forward. "Ms. English, I'm confident that a mistake was made. I'd like to urge you to take a look at my application again."

With the use of her name, Ms. English seemed to soften. "Well, the vice president makes all the final decisions," she said. "But I can take a look and tell you what happened with your application."

"I'd really appreciate it," Todd said, with great relief. Well, his people skills had gotten him this far. Now everything was going to be cleared up, and he'd be rocking that internship all summer.

After he'd listened to Kenny G for a minute or two again, Ms. English came back on the line. Her tone had changed appreciably, and she was now cool, brusque, and firm again.

"Mr. Wilkins, are you currently enrolled at Sweet Valley University?" she asked.

Todd's stomach collapsed. *Oh, no.* "No," he said. "But did you see my business proposal? I took off the semester to further implement some of my ideas in an actual—"

"Mr. Wilkins, this is an internship for a *college* student," Ms. English swiftly cut in. "We are a *corporate* environment. We work with *college* students so that we can *hire* them on graduation. Do you understand?"

Todd felt like he had swallowed one of his pizza boxes whole. "I understand," he whispered.

"Very well, then. Good day," Ms. English said, and hung up the phone. Todd simply stared at the receiver, dumbfounded. He started to have a little feeling that those other rejections might not be mistakes after all.

No, it wasn't turning out to be a good day for Todd—not at all.

Sam sat on the bed in his room, staring dully at the row of CDs in front of him. Pulp. Third Eye Blind. Smashing Pumpkins. Led Zeppelin.

Except for Led Zeppelin—a holdover from fifth grade—all of those titles were pretty accurate descriptions of his emotions right now.

He didn't know what the hell was wrong with him. He'd been aching over Elizabeth Wakefield ever since the first time he met her, with her beautiful blond hair, her clear blue-green eyes, and her sweet, curving smile. He had never met a girl so naked, so free of artifice—so *honest*. Being with her was like listening to a song and needing to go out and buy the album *right then;* like suddenly, after eight weeks of boredom, understanding what the professor was talking about. It was what everyone in life looked for; what everyone, whether they knew it or not, was waiting for. So what was his problem?

Well, the problem was that he was absolutely freaked out. He'd expected to feel calm, relieved, and totally happy when he and Elizabeth finally got together. Instead he felt like he was starting finals week without having studied at all—which, actually, he was. Was everyone better prepared than he was? And was he going to screw everything up again?

No way, Burgess, he told himself, balling up his hands and holding his head in them. When he'd disowned his parents, he'd known that he was leaving for something better, not for failure and the same kind of coldheartedness that made his life with his family so terrible. Now was the chance to make good on his promise.

But how was he supposed to do that when he felt like someone had stuck his brain in the Cuisinart and microwaved his heart?

He was reminding himself of his father. Night after night, his father had returned from work, retreated immediately into his study, polished off a series of gin and tonics, and emerged only for dinner, which he ate silently, his jaw popping when he chewed.

His mother's job had been to handle the house, and she'd done so well, ruling over a series of maids like General Colin Powell with a feather duster. She'd thrown the cocktail parties, presided over Thanksgivings and Easters with her hair perfectly coiffed, her nails keyed to her lipsticks. The house was perfectly decorated, filled with fine china, antiques, and furniture. And you could tell Mr. and Mrs. Burgess secretly detested every second they had to spend in it with each other.

He opened his front desk drawer and reached underneath some papers. Finding one corner of the stiff cardboard rectangle, he withdrew a picture of his family that he hadn't looked at in months. His mother, father, and brother smiled stiffly back at him. He sat in the lower-left corner, his face completely closed, like a door. God, he had left to stop being that guy.

He heard someone stomping down the stairs. He hoped this whole thing wouldn't be more than he could handle because if anyone was worth the trouble, it was Elizabeth. Placing his headphones over his ears, he pumped up the volume on his Walkman and began to hop up and down to Chumbawumba, trying to work out some of the tension. *Let it not be bad, let it not be bad, let it not be bad,* he began chanting to himself. *Whoa, that's really positive,* he realized. *Let it be good, let it be good, let it be good,* he began to chant instead.

Through his headphones he heard a knock on the door. "Can I come in?" he heard Elizabeth say.

"Yeah," he called back, feeling like he was fifteen and going on his first date.

The door opened, and suddenly Elizabeth stood there, wearing some kind of a sleeveless minidress. Her hair had been blown out (even Sam could tell—usually she just let it air dry) so that it hung against her face like a shining curtain, and she was wearing makeup—lots of makeup—on her normally shiny-scrubbed face. On her feet were strappy sandals, and she was clutching some kind of a beaded purse.

It's not that Sam didn't think she looked good. Elizabeth would look beautiful in pigtails and a paper sack. It was just that he wasn't used to seeing her so . . . done up. She not only looked like a different girl; she looked like a different *type* of girl. She looked like the kind of girl whose career goal was to announce the news on MTV or marry some computer wizard and spend her days shopping and talking on her cell phone. She looked like . . . Jessica.

"Hey, you look great," he finally managed to croak. Inwardly he slapped himself on the forehead. Now how was he ever going to manage to explain to Elizabeth that if he'd wanted the fashion-maven twin, he'd have gone for Jessica?

"Thanks," Elizabeth said softly. She held out her arm, and he took it. Even done up, she was still her old self: direct, no BS. Or did the rules change once that girl was wearing eye makeup and spangly eye shadow? Sam didn't know.

"Ready for breakfast?" Elizabeth asked.

Sam nodded rapidly and turned his baseball cap around so that it cast a dark shadow over his eyes. He wasn't going to be the guy in the photograph anymore, but he didn't know *who* he was going to be just yet.

In other words, breakfast, he felt, was the *only* thing he could safely say he was ready for.

Elizabeth could have floated out of the house, she was so elated. For the first time since she was in junior high, she had had a genuine desire to get all dolled up (she had occasionally submitted to her sister's magic M•A•C wand). Something about the feelings Sam had awakened in her made her feel like she needed to show them off—*right away*. She hoped her glam look wasn't causing Sam's complete and total silence as they headed toward Yum-Yums.

Looking at the side of Sam's face, Elizabeth could tell that he was totally scared, whatever other reaction he was having to her *Vogue*-ification. She tried not to let it bother her. That's just how men were, she was realizing: paralyzed, frozen, and terrified until you melted them with your warmth and they became comfortable enough to relax too. She just had to bide her time. The ones you should watch out for were the confident, snappy players like Finn Robinson, Elizabeth thought. Like with first-time drivers, the ones to be scared of were the ones who *weren't* scared.

Elizabeth snuck another look at the silent, ruminative Sam. She knew what she was about to say was corny, but it was so true, she couldn't hold herself back. "Isn't it a beautiful day?" she said, simultaneously thinking, *If Sam can't stand my cheesy side, it's better if I find out right now.* It had rained in the night, and the sky was washed clean, filling the air with the scent of redwood and pine, Elizabeth's favorite natural perfume.

Luckily Sam didn't seem freaked out by that statement. "Yeah," he said, grinning back at her. "Yeah, it really is."

Elizabeth inwardly gave a sigh of relief. "I'm so psyched for the summer," she said. "I've had enough of winter for a hundred years."

Sam looked a little freaked out at the mention of summer, but when he saw Elizabeth wasn't talking about *them* and the summer, he smiled again. Taking Elizabeth's hand, he plucked a blossom from a tree and, brushing her hair behind her ear, placed the flower in her hair. Elizabeth's knees almost buckled at his touch.

"There," Sam said. "Billie Holiday's got nothing on you."

Elizabeth knew how much Sam liked the sultry singer and made a mental note to get him a CD for his birthday.

"I wish," Elizabeth said. "I can't sing at all."

"Well, you're a damn good journalist." Sam laughed. "And makeup artist."

Elizabeth blanched, then laughed back. "Watch it, Mr. My-girlfriend's-an-Ivory-girl," she said. "Or I'll start wearing makeup like this every day."

At the mention of the word *girlfriend*, Elizabeth gulped, and Sam stiffened perceptibly. *God, Elizabeth, do you think you could keep your foot out of your mouth for ten seconds?* she thought. Both of them tried to play it off by pretending it had never happened. Sam even put forth a nonchalant whistle and took her hand again, making Elizabeth sigh with relief—again (for the second time in ten minutes!). She decided to give conversation another try.

"Have you started studying for finals yet?" she asked.

Sam gave her an odd look. "Of course," he said. "They start at OCC this week too."

Why did I say it that way? Elizabeth silently queried herself. Of course. She had been so upset about Sam these past few weeks, finals were like some dim, distant notion in the future, not the very real threat that was now upon her. *Ugh*. Now Sam was going to know that *he* had been the main thing she had been studying around the house, not her notes from her Journalism and the Law class.

"You're not gearing up to flunk everything, Wakefield, are you?" Sam asked her. Elizabeth turned to look and saw that he was flashing her a toothy grin. She calmed down.

"I was thinking I'd try out the seven-year plan," she joked, referring to the students who hung around SVU so long working in coffee shops or in bars that they became minor legends, an extra incentive for incoming freshmen or students suffering from senior slump to hit the books.

When the two reached Yum-Yums, Elizabeth caught a glance of them, holding hands, in the reflection of the glass window. They both looked relaxed and happy—like they'd been together for years instead of hours. Ironic, since clearly both she and Sam were shaking in their boots.

Sam broke the image of the happy couple by holding open the door for Elizabeth. She curtsied and smiled before she walked in, something that she hadn't done since she and Jessica starred in the kiddie-ballet production of *Sleeping Beauty*. Sam's face turned the color of a toilet-paper roll, and he hurried to the front to get them a booth.

What was wrong with her? She never acted like this, especially not with Sam, Mr. Supercool. His ninety-year-old was bringing out her twelve-year-old. She really had to cool it with the cutesy-girl stuff—yesterday.

Chapter Five

Chloe descended the steps of the bus, breathing in the smell of exhaust mixed with french-fry fumes. The mall! Since she was a young girl shopping with her mother, the sight of rows and rows of parked cars, revolving doors, and huge, sky-high signs like Nordstrom and Bloomingdale's had called to her that she was finally, at long last, home.

That didn't mean she had known what she was doing fashionwise, however. Shopping with Mom had always meant preppy, expensive outfits that Chloe had never felt comfortable in. When she'd arrived at SVU, she'd changed her image. The new Chloe wore thrift-store finds, low-slung, baggy jeans, and tattered T-shirts. She'd liked being more herself, but it hadn't exactly won her the admiring eye of any hot guys. After today, though, Chloe would have an entire closetful of trendy, sexy, revealing new clothes.

And her rich parents would be only too happy to receive the bill.

First Chloe hit Banana Republic, which was usually dependable for a slinky sweater or two. Chloe tried on one or two of the fuzzy mohair cropped cardigans with a floor-length silk cargo skirt and looked at herself in the three-way mirror. *Eh.* This was a great look—for a twenty-nine-year-old. She was trying to find a boyfriend, not a job.

Next she plowed through the racks at Express. This was way, way more her speed. Lycra tops . . . fuchsia minis . . . Indian embroidered shirts—bingo! Chloe paired a V-necked top with paisley trim on the collar and cuffs with some boot-cut black pants, then tried the top in acid green with a pink miniskirt. Which outfit looked better? Chloe flipped the tags, then shrugged. Cheapo. She could get both in every color and not feel guilty.

The makeup counter called. Chloe usually was a Rite-Aid girl: One or two Revlon items, a pack of elastics, and she moved on to the detergent aisle. But the shiny tubes and exotic lipstick containers on Nina's bureau top had filled her with the desire to own a collection like that herself. Those secret paints and unguents could spin a guy's head around fast.

Chloe headed for the Stila counter first. Picking among the shiny, stubby tubes, she rubbed a maroon shimmer on her lips. "Wait, that's way too dark on you," the tall, redheaded salesgirl—wearing a gray tag that said Pam—inserted impatiently. Whipping out from behind the counter, she looked at her watch, then at the almost empty makeup court. "It's slow," she said. "I'll do you for free."

Holding Chloe's hair out of her face with a steel banana clip, the salesgirl—who was dressed in knee-high boots, fishnet tights, and some corded black minidress that made Chloe's heart pound with envy—dumped Prescriptives, Chanel, M•A•C, and Stila products on the counter, along with an assortment of brushes and pencils. "We're not supposed to mix and match," she hissed, "but you're so cute, I want to do you up well."

Brandishing a foundation brush (a whole new product that Chloe had to get, Pam informed her), the makeup artist went to work. Chloe felt a variety of products—cold, gooey, slick, powdery—go over her bare skin. "Blend, blend, blend," Pam hummed to herself while she worked. "That's the secret." She also explained to Chloe how to apply each product as she was doing so. Chloe listened like she was hearing the directions to a buried treasure.

If this was the secret to getting guys, she was way past ready to be let in on it already. Pam's face looked flawless—white, smooth skin; green eyes lined with kohl; and a wet, shimmering mouth that looked bare and totally made up at the same time. Chloe didn't fail to notice how the men who passed by—what were *they* doing in the makeup section anyway?—often turned around to get a second look.

After about five minutes Pam whipped Chloe's chair around. "Okay, look," Pam said.

Chloe did a double take. It wasn't that she didn't look like herself—Pam had, thankfully, not slapped one of those scary kabuki masks on her face. But she looked like an infinitely cooler, older, more fabulous version of Chloe—one that Chloe had never believed was lurking under the boring auburn hair and unplucked eyebrows.

Pam was nodding in approval and snapping her gum. "Cool, huh?" she said.

Chloe turned away from the mirror. "You're a genius," she said.

"No, it's your bone structure," Pam demurred, returning behind the counter and propping herself up on her chin. "And you can do it yourself at home—it's really easy."

Chloe leaned across the counter and planted a kiss on the surprised—but game—Pam's cheek. Pam gave Chloe a thank-you hug. "I'll take *every-thing*," Chloe squealed.

Two minutes later and over a hundred dollars poorer, a much more confident Chloe left makeup land and headed straight for a store she'd certainly never gone into with her mother: Victoria's Secret. Almost hyperventilating from excitement, she entered the pink-and-white sanctuary and immediately gathered an armful of silky bras and panties, all in a rainbow of pastels. In the dressing room Chloe was thrilled to realize that the lingerie worked a similar transformation to the makeup: in the slick, skimpy bra-and-panties sets she looked like the archetypal hot, young coed, not a member of the drill team. Spinning around to look at herself from every angle in the mirrors, Chloe drank in the image, putting her hands over her mouth in excitement.

After about three minutes of narcissistic delight a salesgirl knocked. "How are you doing?" she asked.

"Great!" said Chloe, slipping off the most fantastic of her finds: a scandalous mint green bra.

"Well, try this guy," the salesgirl said, holding a handful of bras over the partition. "These just came in today—they're great for the girls with a little less on top, like us."

Chloe scowled to herself but took the handful anyway. "Less" on top. How nice to know that the salesgirls were so considerate in here.

"You pull the string in the center, and it—"

"Thanks, I got it," Chloe said faintly, cutting her off. She put on the first one and began to pull the string that hung down the center. The harder you pulled it, the more cleavage you created.

Chloe watched herself go from ironing board to Charo in three seconds flat.

"You like?" the salesgirl called over.

"I'll take one in every color," Chloe answered.

"Neil, I don't know what I'm going to do," Jessica wailed.

How about breathing into a paper bag? Neil wanted to say. *Or putting one over your head?* he thought of adding snarkily.

Neil was always sympathetic to Jessica up to a point, but that point had been crossed long ago. These roommates were just ridiculous: a trial a second. His tenure in this house had been canceled, and he had found a summer and junior-year replacement. Leave the Macbeth and Lady Macbeths in training to work out their internecine squabbles by themselves.

"Why don't you start by calming down," he said gently.

Jessica spun on him, her eyes blazing. "My sister's dating a jerk *in my house*, and you tell me to calm down. Great advice, Neil," she spat.

Neil took his legs off his desk and put them down on the floor with a bang. Being sympathetic (up to a point) was one thing; being yelled at in one's own room was entirely another. Jessica had crossed a line. She was totally rude, inconsiderate, and much too loud—especially when he had an Early American History final tomorrow morning.

"Jess, it's Elizabeth's house as much as it's yours," Neil reminded her impatiently. "And mine and Sam's too, for that matter." He racked his brain, trying to come up with an impression of Jessica that would be unpleasant enough to get her to drop this whole thing. Finally he found it. "You're not Elizabeth's chaperon, you know."

Jessica sat on the bed, her pale pink fingernails curling deeply into the coverlet. "So you *approve* of this relationship?" she hissed.

Neil threw down a pencil in frustration. What was wrong with Jessica—didn't she see the pile of *books* in front of him? The open pad and highlighter? The get-lost-I'm-studying pack of Tab and M&M's by his right arm?

"It's not my place to approve or disapprove," Neil said, trying to remain calm by tapping the pink highlighter against the desktop. "Nor yours, for that matter."

Jessica was up again, her arms crossed, pacing. "What do you mean, not my *place?*" she yelled. "I'm her *twin,* for heaven's sake. We were once *one* egg."

And you've become a goose, Neil wanted to say. "You might as well be her great-grandaunt for all the right that gives you to butt in to her sex life," he said curtly.

Jessica shot him a look. "Well, I'm not going to let her get hurt again," she snapped bitterly. "I hope my friends would do the same for me in her situation."

Jessica, you have no idea exactly what some of your friends would like to do to you right this moment, Neil thought. Thinking of stupendously sarcastic responses to annoying situations always made him feel better eventually. He tried to be more generous, hoping that would shoo Jessica back into her own room. "Well, seeing as you're not likely to start dating Sam anytime soon," he said dryly, "I'll just file that comment away."

"Elizabeth is totally going down the slippery slope," Jessica ranted, sounding like the heroine of a terrible B movie. "And I've got to stop her."

Neil stood up and put his hands on her shoulders. "You've just got to stop," he said, trying to seem supportive. "Elizabeth is a smart cookie, and this is her own business. Leave it alone."

Jessica was looking across the room with a horrified expression on her face. What now? Had she developed the power to see through walls and caught a glimpse of Sam and Elizabeth canoodling somewhere on campus?

"Oh, no!" she shrieked, and slapped her forehead. Neil turned to look at the pink-and-turquoise deco clock on his far wall. "My art final! I'm totally gonna miss it!"

Gathering up her books and papers in a sloppy handful, Jessica booked out of the room and down the hall. A minute later he heard the front door slam. The silence, after Tornado Jessica, was sublime.

His roommates clearly had a whole Aaron Spelling thing going on, but that didn't mean he needed to replace Dylan for the season finale. He would continue to give advice to Jessica—from a safe distance. That check he had given to Mona wasn't only for his rent. It was a down payment on his sanity.

Jessica sprinted out of Neil's room, her irritation at his lack of support only mitigated by the pure fear that ran through her veins at the thought of being late for her art-history final. Professor Greenfield never hesitated to single out students for questions during her lectures just as they were nodding off or to lock the main door one minute into class so that tardy students were forced to slink around to the entrance in the front of the auditorium, where the entire lecture hall would watch them slump into their seats in embarrassment.

Jessica had had that experience once at the beginning of the semester, and that had been enough.

Puffing as she ran along the crowded path cutting through the main part of campus, Jessica realized that Professor Greenfield probably wouldn't even leave that front door open today. "I'm sorry, Ms. Wakefield," Jessica could just hear her saying while Jessica lamely stood above her desk, trying to offer a series of increasingly desperate excuses. "But explain to me again why it was impossible for you to arrive at my final on time, as did your classmates? The roads were not flooded out, I presume."

Lost in the horrific fantasy, Jessica tripped on a mislaid piece of paving stone and flew into a full-body dive, sprawling over the path while her books and papers flipped everywhere. She let out a strangled sound, wanting to burst into tears of frustration.

"Hey, are you all right?" a familiar-looking guy asked, extending his hand. Jessica stood up, rubbing off her jeans and cursing as he knelt down and began to gather her books for her. "That's all right," Jessica said gratefully, joining him once she ascertained that she hadn't sustained any sizable wounds in her nosedive. "I can get these."

"Jessica, it's no problem," the guy said, flashing a killer grin. Jessica finally remembered who he was: Clyde, the junior on the diving team whom she had flirted with at a series of parties her freshman year. Why hadn't anything ever happened with him?

"So, uh," he said, once they were both standing, "where ya been this year?"

In purgatory, Jessica answered silently, wondering if she looked as heinous as she felt. "Clyde, I'd love to talk," she said hurriedly, "but I'm so close to being locked out of my art-history final."

"Oh, Greenfield, huh?" Clyde responded sympathetically. "Well, see you around, I hope."

I hope he didn't think I was blowing him off, Jessica thought as she blasted through the swinging doors that led into the main art building. She broke into a flat sprint down the wide, curving hallway, then grasped the steel door handle just as another hand on the inside was pulling it firmly shut. Giving the door an extra yank, she found herself face-to-face with a bemused Professor Greenfield, who inclined her head very slightly to the left as she regarded her quivering student. "Well, we thank you for taking the trouble to come by, Ms. Wakefield," she said, loud enough for the students sitting in the upper rows to hear every word. "I hope it wasn't too harsh a burden to ask that you grace us with your presence for the final day of the course," she added, smiling ruthlessly.

"Not at all," Jessica muttered. Face burning with shame, she took a seat as close to the door as possible, wishing that she could dissolve into the sunbeam causing a halo around the seats in the

71

row in front of her. *Well, you can never say I didn't learn the principles of aesthetics this term,* she thought ruefully.

Jessica felt an elbow jostle her own. "You're bleeding," a voice hissed.

Jessica turned to her left. It was Brett, the tall lacrosse player who had peppered her with calls a couple of months ago, when she and Neil were fighting over what's-his-name—Jason. Jessica had totally forgotten about him too. *When did I become a tourist in my own love life?* she wondered.

"Thanks," Jessica whispered, blotting the wound with the edge of her shirt. This disaster with her sister was certainly taking her grooming standards down a notch or two.

Brett silently reached into his pocket and handed her a freshly washed handkerchief as the teaching assistants fanned out into the room, dispensing stacks of blue books and exams down every row. Jessica gratefully pressed it against her elbow. It was barely eleven, and all of these Prince Charmings were suddenly coming out of the woodwork. For the first time Jessica felt genuinely grateful for the male attention instead of simply supremely worthy, as usual. She smiled at Brett again.

"The blue books are coming your way," he whispered, pointing over Jessica's shoulder. Jessica jumped and turned to her left, taking one from the stack and passing it on.

"Sorry," she whispered back.

"Ms. Wakefield, would you and your seat partner like to retire to a private room?" Professor Greenfield called from the front of the auditorium. Jessica fervently wished that she had actually been locked out of the exam, regardless of the F it would have earned her. It was turning out to be a red-letter day for public humiliation, it seemed.

Brett nudged her again. *"You bet,"* he had written in large type on the front of his blue book. He smiled slyly at her as he turned over his pencil to erase it.

Jessica's heart melted. It had been so long, she realized, since she'd obsessed about some guy who was into her instead of one that Elizabeth was into.

"And . . . begin," Professor Greenfield intoned, watching the second hand of her slim, brushed-steel, legendary blue-face Rolex with an eagle eye.

Jessica turned to her blue book, her mounting panic giving way to only minor distress as she realized she knew most of the short identification questions. Accepting a Bic from Brett when her own pen began to ink all over the pages (and her hand), Jessica plunged into the essay portion.

Sam should be here to see how a gentleman really *treats a woman,* Jessica thought bitterly as she scrawled through pages of blue-lined paper, Sam's sarcastic, sullen face drifting in front of her mind's eye. Okay, maybe she was being a little too obsessive with her worry about Elizabeth hooking up with Sam. But Jessica had just seen Elizabeth get her heart crushed by that jerk Finn Robinson, who'd only been interested in one thing, which, thank God, he hadn't gotten. Granted, Sam had been uncharacteristically helpful to Elizabeth when her heart had been ripped out. But the minute Elizabeth had actually expected something from Sam, like, oh, maturity, Sam had flown the coop and had been caught in some serious lies.

Why was Elizabeth willing to forget all that to suck face with the jerk? Didn't her sister realize she was setting herself up for a summer of heartache? Sam was beneath her in every way! It had to be that Elizabeth felt she couldn't trust the supposedly perfect-appearing guys, like Finn, to be the real thing. That must be why she was betting on a slacker like Sam.

Maybe I should bring Brett and Clyde by the house and set up a Manwich exhibition so both Sam and Elizabeth can get a clue.

Looking up frantically at the clock as she struggled to finish the last essay question, Jessica couldn't believe she had exactly two seconds left.

"And . . . time," Professor Greenfield called

crisply, dispatching her claque of TAs to collect the exams from the rows of scribbling students.

Jessica frantically scanned her last essays, making sure she had included all of the historical footnotes and theoretical glosses Professor Greenfield had peppered her famous lectures with all semester. As Jessica came to the last couple of pages, her stomach tightened. *Omigod,* she screamed inwardly. She was so out of it, she had scribbled a diatribe about Sam to Elizabeth on the last couple of pages, interspersing analytical prose with gems like, *He's such a commitmentphobic, lying jerk, Liz! What are you thinking?*

Before she knew it, the student to her left had plucked the exam out of her hand, reaching over her to take the passed-over stack from Brett while the FBI-agent-like TA stamped his foot impatiently. Jessica put her head in her hands. Immediately Brett leaned over.

"What's wrong?" he whispered.

It's over, Jessica said to herself. *You've finally cracked. Psychiatrist city.*

"Hey, you wanna go get a coffee or something?" Brett asked. "You look pretty on the edge."

Jessica took her hands off her face and gave him a wan smile. Little did he know that clearly she had overshot the edge and gone clear around the bend a long, long time ago.

* * *

Todd snapped up his head, trying to not let the Muzak he was forced to listen to while on hold for his last-choice company lull him into the sleep he so greatly craved. He didn't know whether to start throwing things against the wall or lock himself in his closet: Every single company he had called— even the ones from whom he hadn't received official rejection notices from yet—had had the same reaction. Not in college? Can't work here. *Click.*

Without noticing it, Todd slowly began to drift off toward sleep. As his head went back against his pillows, his hand gently replaced the receiver in its cradle. His mouth hung open, and he began to gently snore. The Muzak-ified version of "Livin' la Vida Loca" continued to drift through his head, coloring his dream with the frenetic pace of a music video.

In his dream Todd was in what had become a very typical setting: Frankie's, around closing time. As he often did, he finished the paperwork, then reached over to the taps to pour himself a beer. In the dream, however, the first one—Bass— was empty. Dream Todd reacted pretty much as real Todd would have: with extreme irritation. He pushed down the series of taps one by one, his panic mounting as nothing happened. They were all empty! What the hell was going on?

Then, as dream Todd was going over in his

head all the possible causes, every single tap began to run simultaneously. Todd joyfully reached over to push them closed, then began to panic again as he realized he couldn't. Pushing against the taps with all his might, he tried to stop the tide of beer swilling around his ankles while he calculated how much pay he was going to lose for this snafu.

In the dream Frankie's became filled with beer as quickly as if all the taps were fire hoses. Before he knew it, Todd was floating somewhere up near the ceiling, thinking, *If I drown in this, it's going to be nowhere near as romantic as when Leonardo DiCaprio died in* Titanic. Taking a deep breath, dream Todd flipped down and began to swim through the golden beer, trying to lift the catch on the old paned windows and push himself to freedom. As he struggled with the metal brackets, Todd saw that—weirdly—his parents, Elizabeth, Jessica, Dana, and Tom Watts were all watching him from outside as if through a fishbowl, shouting something frantically and gesturing wildly with their hands. *What are they doing here?* he thought, still pulling on the window latches with all his might—which, in the dream, seemed pretty puny. And what were they saying to him? Was it to *break* something? *Brake* or *break*? And break what?

Chapter
Six

"Let me get that for you," Sam said, pulling out the chair as Elizabeth approached the table.

"Chivalry lives," Elizabeth said, immediately kicking herself once again. From zero to snappish in three seconds. Who was this cheerleader-slash-shrew who had overtaken her body? *Argh!*

Sam grinned, still looking nervous. Elizabeth wondered why—*was* it something she was doing? If she stopped being so schizophrenic, would he relax? But maybe that wasn't a good idea. The last months they had both been relaxed, and they had nearly torn each other to shreds like wild animals.

"Well, chivalry and privacy," Sam responded, pulling up his chair catty-corner to Elizabeth's so that they were bracketed into their own private corner. "I want to tell you something."

Please don't let him be ending things already,

Elizabeth thought. After her experience with Finn, no amount of frightening behavior from the male species could surprise her.

"We've never really had the chance to sit down and talk about what happened two months ago, Liz," Sam said. "A lot of stuff happened, but the most important thing I want you to know is, I didn't lie to you." Sam cupped his hands on the tabletop and looked down at them. "I omitted things, it's true, but I didn't lie."

Elizabeth knew they were talking about the million-dollar question: why Sam had claimed to be totally broke, too broke even to afford SVU, when, from what Elizabeth had uncovered, he was more like the son of Donald Trump. She was thrilled that he was bringing up this touchy subject, but she wasn't going to let him off the hook so easily. "Well, you omitted the most salient piece of information, Sam," she said, trying not to sound too much like Judge Judy.

Sam took in a whistling breath, then exhaled deeply. "It wasn't about *not* telling you. My parents *are* rich. But that doesn't make *me* rich. It hasn't made me rich ever since I disowned them." Sam leaned back in his chair. "And I really haven't talked about—or with—them since."

Elizabeth just looked at Sam for a moment: He was obviously in great agony. Should she just leave well enough alone? She decided to press it just a little bit further. This wound was going to fester if he didn't open it up a little bit.

"Do you ever talk about why you disowned them?" Elizabeth asked, using the classic psychological distancing technique she had perfected for her difficult interviews.

Sam shot her a look. "It's a long story," he said slowly, indicating with his tone that it wasn't one he was going to be ready to tell Elizabeth Wakefield anytime soon. "I'd rather not go there right now," he added, just in case she hadn't taken the hint.

Elizabeth had taken it, but she also didn't want to lose the small headway she'd made. If she was too apologetic, she knew from experience, Sam would close the door forever on the topic, and she'd never be able to wiggle her way back into his confidence again. "You don't have to tell me right now if you don't want to," she said. "But when you're ready, I want to hear the story. Sam, I—" She caught herself just in time. *Sam, I love you,* had almost tumbled out of her mouth like a pile of dead fish onto a dock.

"You what?" Sam said, looking defensive. Clearly he had no idea what she'd been about to say. And neither had she before it had almost slipped out! Did she really *love* Sam? How could you love someone that you'd only just officially gotten together with the night before?

If you didn't count hundreds of fantasies, that was. Thank God, Sam thought she was about to say, "Sam, I deserve to know," or something equally officious and annoying. In this situation she preferred Sam thinking she was brutally inconsiderate to knowing that she was in *love*.

"I really . . . c-care about you," Elizabeth managed to stutter. *Well, that's really original, Wakefield,* she thought. Still, it was better than nothing. She couldn't tell Sam she loved him—not for a long while, she realized. If she wanted Sam to stay firmly planted in the seat across from her and not bolt from the place, terrified, it had to be baby steps all the way. *Well, patience supposedly is a virtue,* she thought, smiling.

Sam looked up shyly, a slow blush darkening his face. "I care about you too, Elizabeth," he said haltingly. She couldn't believe how human he was being.

Elizabeth beamed back. A server approached and placed the little blackboard menus on their table, scurrying away before they could even put in orders for regular coffee. "Will you go with me to SVU's semiformal?" Elizabeth burst out before she could stop herself.

Sam glanced down at the menu. "Yeah, okay," he said, only a little stiffly.

"Great," Elizabeth said, excitement mixing with the twinge of insecurity that bloomed every time Sam winced or looked uncomfortable at one of her stabs at intimacy. *It's not about you, Elizabeth,* she reminded herself. *Remember that.*

Sam looked up from his menu. "You ready?"

Elizabeth looked him straight in the eye. "I am. Are you?"

As Sam and Elizabeth left Yum-Yums, he was grateful that after their muffins and mocchacinos had arrived, the interrogation had ended. Being with Elizabeth, he was just beginning to realize, often felt like he had become the prisoner in one of those movies where the guy was placed in a room and questioned by a series of smoking men with accents while a harsh, bright light was shined in his eyes. Sam could almost see the *whomp* of the floodlight being turned on in Elizabeth's eyes as they lit up during questioning.

"What're you thinking?" Elizabeth asked, scrutinizing him in a friendly way.

"Nothing much," he said, grabbing her hand to appease her. God, she was so intense! Every twitch, every blink, every muscle twitch was being analyzed and filed away for future examination.

Elizabeth squeezed back. *This is so weird,* he thought. Just yesterday he had—if he was honest with himself—wanted to put a piece of tape over her mouth so she could never speak again. But today, when he looked at her, what he mostly felt was amazement that she had consented to walk around with him and an astonishingly warm glow at her very presence. She was like a shot of adrenaline or something. Had all of those bad feelings just been because he had thought he could never be with her? That she disliked him so much, she would never even bother to be civil?

"Well, Zen masters work very hard at being able to think of nothing," Elizabeth joked. "You must be a very advanced being."

Sam smiled back, but underneath the smile he was thinking how much he disliked it that Elizabeth always implied that he must, of course, be thinking of something very serious. Well, okay—he was. But why did she have to let him know that *she* knew? Was it supposed to make him open up more? Because it made him want to snap shut like a clam and drift to the bottom of the ocean.

"I played a lot of Nintendo as a child," he said, trying to be as light as Elizabeth so she wouldn't suspect that he was in mild agony. "That greatly improved my powers of concentration."

"Ooh," Elizabeth said, squeezing his hand again. "We weren't allowed to have Nintendo—or cable—until Steven started to recite the phone book at the table since he'd gone through every book in the house, including a stack of old *National Geographics*. When we reached the F's, Mom and Dad finally relented."

Why was she telling him this—so he could see just how messed up his stick-him-in-front-of-the-TV family was in comparison to hers? Or was she trying to show him the type of firm-but-loving behavior she expected from him in the future? It seemed weird for her to spin amusing family yarns when he had just confessed the mildly important fact that he no longer even spoke to the people that had given him food (well, caviar) and shelter (more like a mansion) for eighteen years.

Whoa, buddy, she's just making conversation, the saner part of his brain put in. *Put the rattling saber away.*

"It just blows my mind that you could have a really persistent sibling," he said, accessing the humorous part of his brain instead of the wildly paranoid one. "I mean, I would have seen your family as a bunch of meek, unprepossessing types."

"Ha ha," Elizabeth said dryly, giving his hand another squeeze. This was so extreme. Was this what it was like to be with someone? Was that even what he wanted?

Just a day ago he had wanted to tumble off the

edge of the earth and take this girl with him. Now evidently he and Elizabeth had gotten on line for the Tunnel of Love, he was cracking jokes right and left like Chris Rock, and he had to rent some tux for a big-deal dance. Rolling with the punches, he knew, wasn't one of his strong points. Were you supposed to discover entirely new facets of yourself when you started seeing someone? Was the gorgeous girl next to you supposed to seem like a cross between Pamela Anderson Lee (minus the fake boobs) and a boa constrictor? As if sensing his thoughts, Elizabeth grinned wickedly and gave his hand another squeeze.

Well, Sam thought, squeezing back, *I'll have to wait and see.*

Chapter Seven

Chloe shifted from side to side so that her handfuls of bags didn't make her keel over one way or the other. This stupid bus was taking so long to come! It must be nearly three o'clock, Chloe thought, looking at the position of the sun against the tenplex in one corner of the mall.

The bus finally chugged up, spewing exhaust in all directions. Chloe straggled into line behind two teenage boys (what were they doing out of school anyway? Was this their spring break? High school seemed like *so long ago*) and maneuvered her way up the steps, plopping the heap of bags right under the bus driver's nose as she fumbled in her pockets for change.

"Big night out, eh?" the woman cracked, enjoying the spectacle of Chloe's discomfort.

"Sure," Chloe said, letting the last nickel rattle

into the slot. Why was everyone always sticking their noses into her business? Did the whole world need to establish that Chloe was a dateless, flat-chested loser on a daily basis?

But once she sat down and shoved all her bags under the seat, Chloe cheered up. She really had seen a whole new side of herself in Pam's chair. And she truly did look hot in her new clothes—*brutally* hot. Guys were going to want to hang pictures of her on their walls like she was Giselle or Catherine Zeta-Jones or something.

The bus pulled up to the next stop, and Chloe became lost in her fantasy—honestly, how cool would it be to walk through campus and have a path make itself? To have messages on her machine every day from guys, with things like, "Um, I saw you across the quad today, and I was just wondering . . ."? To have the next freshman class's girls point at her enviously, whispering how beautiful she was? To have guys lining up to get her drinks at keg parties?

"Excuse me," Chloe heard, as if from a thousand miles away. She looked up. An older woman in a button-front coat and hat, just as loaded up with shopping bags as Chloe, gestured at the seat next to Chloe's, where Chloe had piled up all of her bags.

"I'd like to sit here, if you don't mind," the woman said.

"I don't mind," said Chloe. From campus queen to annoying teenager was a long way to fall in two seconds, but Chloe tried not to take it too hard. She put half of the bags on her lap and the other half around her feet while the woman wriggled into some semblance of comfort. With a sigh she collapsed back.

"Now, I hope you don't mind my asking," the woman said, "but what is a young girl like yourself doing shopping at the mall on a school day?"

For a second Chloe didn't even realize the woman was talking to her. "Oh, I'm not in high school," she said brightly. "I'm in college."

The woman nodded sagely. "So tell me," she said. "What is a young college student like you doing shopping at the mall on a school day?"

Chloe tried to let the blankness of her face speak for how intensely she wanted to engage in this conversation. "I have a dance," she said flatly. *What business is this of yours anyway, lady?* she thought in annoyance.

The woman appeared to perk up. That is, she inclined her head slightly in Chloe's direction. "Oh? You have a young man?"

Chloe felt her ears tingle, which always occurred when someone asked her a question she didn't want to answer. "Well, not exactly," she said.

"What, not exactly?" The woman laughed to herself. "You don't know him yet? Or he doesn't know you?"

Chloe felt her entire face flush. "I don't exactly think of it like that," she said.

The woman laughed again and patted Chloe on the knee. "We never do, do we?"

Chloe hunched down in her seat, miserable. The woman began to chat with another older woman seated across from her, thankfully. Chloe began to think of her clothes and immediately felt better. Once she put on her new shirts and makeup, no one would ever humiliate her this way. People would treat her like . . . like a *woman*. Chloe tried to imagine people calling her a "woman" routinely. She liked the sound of that.

Every time the bus went under an overpass, Chloe caught a glimpse of herself in the window across from her. The first time she saw exactly what everyone else was seeing: a miserable, spindly girl surrounded by shopping bags and bad karma. But by the third or fourth time Chloe got the hang of it. She sat up straight and gathered her hair up on her head with her left hand. Pursing her lips, she waited for her reflection to appear again. There it was! She could swear that this time, she looked kind of like the younger sister of Calista Flockhart.

She felt an elbow in her side. "Young lady," the older woman said, looking with concern at Chloe's pose. "Are you all right?"

"So you're not coming back to the house?" Elizabeth said.

Sam was standing with his backpack on his shoulder, shifting his weight uneasily. He looked toward campus.

"Nah," he said, refusing to meet Elizabeth's eyes directly. "I . . . uh . . . promised I'd meet Bugsy and Floyd at OCC. We've got that bio final."

He needs his space, Elizabeth thought. The chocolate-coconut muffin she'd consumed sat like a tire in her stomach. All of this feinting and retreating: She should have tried out for the fencing team.

"Great," she said, trying to sound happy and like everything was cool. She put her hand on Sam's arm and left it there a second, her throat tightening despite herself. *He's just going to study!* she shrieked to herself. *Get a grip.*

"Hey, I'll make dinner tonight," she burst out. "To celebrate that we're—" Elizabeth mentally slapped her hand over her mouth. She really, really needed to tone it down. She had been about to say, *To celebrate that we're a couple.* Brilliant. That would have put Sam right at ease.

"To celebrate what?" Sam said, looking minorly impatient.

"That we're going to be done with finals soon," Elizabeth put in smoothly. She was getting better at this remove-foot-from-mouth kind of thing.

"Oh, cool," said Sam, looking—Elizabeth couldn't help but see—relieved. He leaned over and nervously gave her a small peck on the cheek. "That would be great. Don't go to too much trouble, though."

Elizabeth experienced a full-body flush. "Okay, see you tonight!" Sam was already backing away. He turned around and gave her a quick wave over his shoulder.

Damn. Still not quite right, really. Elizabeth felt a wave of insecurity. Watching Sam's retreating back, she tried to shrug it off. He was just scared that things were going so fast, she told herself. She had to remember that his needing space—and time—wasn't about her.

Would have been nice to snuggle all day on the couch with their books, though. Mental note: *Get Sam up to speed on snuggling.*

Nina! Talking to Nina would be the perfect transition from Sam mode to study mode. It would also give her the chance to babble all about her evening and morning with Sam—she was *bursting* to talk to somebody about her new love.

Elizabeth hurried to Nina's dorm, hoping that her best friend would be in her regular place by the window and not holed up in some cubbyhole at SVU's library.

Elizabeth stared up at Nina's window. There Nina was, curled up on her window seat, her nose in a textbook. Smiling, Elizabeth headed inside the dorm and practically flew up the stairs.

She stopped at Nina's door and knocked. "Neen? It's me, Liz."

Nina opened the door and smiled too. "It's like a train station or something in here today," she said, taking Elizabeth's backpack from her and dumping it on the floor. She closed her closet door as best she could, considering it was brimming open with all the cardigans Chloe had pulled out.

"Oh, have you been besieged by visitors?" Elizabeth asked, stretching out fully on Nina's bed. She couldn't wait to tell her all about Sam.

"Yeah, Chloe stopped by earlier," Nina said, rolling her eyes. "She's been reading *Cosmo* too much, I think. She seems to have decided that clothes make the woman or something."

Elizabeth looked down at her own minidress, then across at Nina's jeans and T-shirt. At the exact same time they both burst into laughter.

"Okay, so I have something to tell you!"

Elizabeth said, unable to keep her excitement down any longer.

"Omigod, what?" Nina asked, shoving aside a pile of clothes to get on the bed.

Eyes shining, Elizabeth began to lay out all the dreamy details of the evening. First she filled Nina in on the talk that became the major make-out jam. "And he is such an incredible kisser," Elizabeth gushed, unable to keep the thrill out of her voice. Nina didn't look that thrilled back, she noticed.

"You didn't do the full on, did you?" Nina asked.

"No, of course not!" Elizabeth said. What was wrong with Jessica and Nina? "You think I'd go from speaking to the guy for the first time in months to having sex?"

"Good point," Nina said, smiling. "So then what happened?"

"Well, we went to breakfast at Yum-Yums. I was really glad he didn't run off because he was so nervous this morning, I thought he was going to explode," Elizabeth said quickly. "But I think if I just really take it slow—you know, don't push him—things will be okay."

"Uh-huh," Nina said. "And where's Mr. Wonderful now?"

Elizabeth didn't know how to take that, but she assumed Nina wasn't being as sarcastic as she sounded. "He's with Bugsy and Floyd," she said.

"Back to the fold, huh?" Nina said, crossing her arms and narrowing her eyes.

Elizabeth sat up. This was definitely not turning out to be the screamingly joyous new-guy-in-the-house session she had imagined when she booked over here.

"He had to study," Elizabeth said. "It's finals. What's wrong, Nina?"

Nina finally released her face and let go with the full frown she had clearly been holding back the entire time. "Liz, I know how you feel about Sam. That doesn't worry me. You've totally got your head together. What worries me is that it seems like you're letting him off every hook there is. I mean, you take one step toward him, he takes one step back. Doesn't sound like true romance to me." Nina began to tap her foot in an angry staccato.

Elizabeth exhaled. "That's not how it is, Nina," she said. "He's just jumpy, that's all. I mean, does a guy have to hire a limo and send roses every day to pass muster around here or what?"

Instead of backing down, as Elizabeth had hoped, Nina seemed to get even angrier. "Elizabeth, Sam has been jerking you around all year," she said. "Now more than ever he should be sweating your feelings, girl! Don't you see that?"

Elizabeth felt a small twinge of . . . something. But Sam wasn't *ready* to act that way. He'd get there once he calmed down.

"I mean, you're playing possum for Sam. You're trying to hold your tongue for Sam. Sam *should* be sending you a limo and roses every day for a month! Then at least we'd know he was serious," Nina said in a rush.

Elizabeth felt sick. Jessica had been bad enough, but now this. "So you think he's not serious?" she asked quietly.

Nina did finally back down—a little. "Elizabeth, I didn't mean that. I'm sure he has every good intention," she said, finally letting her face open up from its wary look. "But you deserve a boyfriend who thinks about *you*. Who cares how *you* feel. Who you don't have to treat like he's made of china because you're afraid he's going to break."

Elizabeth swallowed. Nina just didn't understand; it was clear. Anyway, she had messed up with all those boys this semester, hadn't she? Did that make her an expert or the last person on earth to listen to? Elizabeth didn't know.

"I hear you, Nina," Elizabeth said stiffly, getting her backpack and standing up. "I should study. Thanks for talking to me about it."

Nina didn't bite and get apologetic, as

Elizabeth had hoped. "I just care about you, Lizzie. I want the best for you. You're my best friend."

Elizabeth felt better. She gave Nina a good-bye hug and walked out of the dorm, her thoughts in turmoil.

I don't want the best, Elizabeth thought as she made her way over to OCC. *I want Sam, whatever he is. Is that so wrong?*

"Whoa, Chloe, *shop* ever?" snickered a popular Theta with a group of friends as Chloe straggled up the steps to the house. The girls laughed.

"Needed a break from cramming for finals," Chloe told her. "You know how it is." She was sure she looked really stunning, with her makeup running off her face from the heat of the bus, loaded down with bags like Julia Roberts in *Pretty Woman*.

"Not a bad idea," another Theta said. "Hey, guys, let's hit the mall. I could definitely use a break."

So now Chloe was a trendsetter. That was something, at least. As she pushed through Theta house's doors, she thought about the celebrities whose sexy looks she wanted to copy. Calista Flockhart. Laura San Giacomo from *Just Shoot Me*. Nia Long. Michelle Williams. Stars who were considered really attractive but didn't have mile-high legs and flaxen hair like most celebs.

As she made her way along the corridor, trying desperately not to let the bags' handles cut off all circulation from her fingers, Deborah, a girl in her lit class, ran up to her, her face frozen in an anxious mask.

"Chloe!" she said, grasping Chloe's arm as if she were drowning. "I am so stressed about the final on Monday. You don't have the notes from the Chekhov lecture, do you?"

Chloe grimaced uneasily, shifting her weight so that she didn't collapse. Deborah evidently was too stressed out to notice and kept her claw on Chloe's arm. "Um, I think I was absent that day," Chloe said. "I can check for you tomorrow or something."

Deborah looked at Chloe like she had just said she was heading off to Aspen to get in some snowboarding on Monday. "You haven't started studying yet?" Deborah said, withdrawing her hand from Chloe's arm like she might be contagious.

"Um, no, I have," Chloe lied, giving up and putting down one or two bags. "I just haven't gotten to Chekhov yet."

"But Chekhov was the third week," Deborah said, like she wasn't sure Chloe spoke English.

What was Deborah, the FBI or something?

"That's not the way I study," Chloe said sweetly, drawing up diplomacy from some vast reserve she had never tapped before. Study, study, study. What was wrong with everyone around here? It was finals, not World War III.

Chloe picked up her bags. "I'm sorry. I gotta go," she said, maintaining her Miss Teen USA smile. "Why don't you come by and pick up those notes tomorrow?"

"Okay," Deborah said faintly. Was that pity or awe in her voice?

As Chloe neared her room, she heard voices rising from the Theta common room.

"Oh, Jan, you are *not* wearing sea foam. That is *so* 1998!"

"Shut up, you hose beast. Who let her boyfriend wear a yellow tux to last year's Spring Fling?"

"Don't go there. Anyway, you're not really wearing that green, are you? It's so . . . pukey."

"I can't believe you said my dress is *pukey*."

They all burst out laughing. They must be talking about the dance, Chloe thought. Her resolve was strengthened. She was going to be there too, she reaffirmed. And she certainly was *not* going to be wearing sea foam.

Dumping her bags on the bed, Chloe dashed off for a quick shower. (Putting all her new clothes and extra makeup over her sweaty body was *not* going to be the look she was going for, she was pretty certain.) When she got back, she laid out all her new clothes in front of her so she could be sure to choose the hottest look imaginable. The skirt? No, too nippy out. It had to be the pants, her new tank top, and the tie-front cardigan. That was basically what Nina had been wearing at the Hot Dog Festival, and Chloe knew that look worked.

Thrilled with her choices, Chloe began to blow out her hair with a round brush, a habit she had perfected long ago but only did occasionally because it took so long. Piling tons of Flat Out goop onto the mass of strands, she went to work, rolling the comb back and forth to make sure she got out every inch of frizz. When her hair started to smell like it might be burning slightly, she turned off the dryer. Perfect. And the heat from blowing out her hair had given her face a nice rosy glow too.

Next Chloe began on her face. First she smeared on tons of foundation, then blended it all into her face with a sponge so you couldn't even see it, like Pam had taught her. Next came some concealer under the eyes to hide the bags she always had. Then a light dusting of powder and blush. The liquid eyeliner was a little more difficult, but Chloe managed, tilting her face up into the mirror and counting to herself very quickly while she drew the line so that she wouldn't blink and stab herself in the eye. After that it was just a little plummy lipstick—applied with a brush!—and a sweep of glimmery shadow on the lids, and she was done. Chloe sat back and looked at herself. Impressive. God, she'd always been okay at art, but who would have known that makeup didn't always have to make you look like that woman on *The Drew Carey Show*?

After Chloe had put on her outfit, she hung a pair of glittering baubles from her ears and put on the pink choker she'd surreptitiously borrowed from Nina. (Nina would be too stuck in her books to notice it was gone before tomorrow anyway.) Some funky barrettes and she was done. She looked at the new-and-improved Chloe in the mirror, shaking her head with disbelief. Jennifer Love Hewitt, watch out.

If this doesn't get me a date, Chloe thought, *I'm a lost cause.*

When Sam had walked away from Elizabeth to head off to OCC, guilt settled on his shoulders, twice as heavy as his backpack, immediately. He really shouldn't have lied to her about heading off to meet Bugsy and Floyd to study for the bio final. That's how losers like Finn got made, wasn't it? Lying to their girlfriends to make things easier? At the thought that he might be like Finn, Sam's stomach curled, and he walked more aggressively along the path, his face clouding, his hands shoved in his pockets.

But then again, he'd had to get away, right? As much as he liked Elizabeth, if he spent the entire day with her, he might not be able to talk to her for weeks. He was the kind of guy that needed to take things *s-l-o-w-l-y*. He would have to work on not holding it against Elizabeth that she was the type of girl who wasn't.

He vaulted up the steps to the library, catching himself just as the swinging doors almost closed, and strode through. Tons of people sat hunched over desks and squeezed in cubbyholes. Jeez! It was finals week, after all. He should be concentrating like everyone else, not hanging around with Elizabeth and having deep, important talks about his childhood. That was his absolute nightmare of life: that a relationship would come and keep him away from doing what he really needed—or just wanted—to do.

As he walked, Sam looked at the other guys he saw around him, all either lounging confidently on the grass, throwing a Frisbee, or striding forward like they were definitely going somewhere. What secret were they in on? Why didn't they worry that a girl was going to eat them alive? Why didn't they have to estrange themselves from their families?

Jeez, Sam, because their families aren't as creepy as yours! he screamed inwardly.

Sam felt a sudden twinge. The last time he had felt that—that desperate, searing urge to run—it had been because his family was choking the life out of him. He hadn't had any choice but to go; it had been lose himself or lose them.

Was Elizabeth treating him like his family had, or was he treating Elizabeth like she was his family?

Ambivalent much? Sam asked himself, feeling less like laughing than like throwing up his hands and taking up residence in the stacks of the library. He passed the crowds of students without seeing them, heading downstairs to the regular place he, Bugsy, and Floyd always used to study. He realized that suddenly he understood why all those men always headed off to the corner bar to be with their friends. They were just trying to get away from their wives. *Is this gonna be the rest of my life?* he thought. *Running away from the girl I'm crazy about? That can't be the only way.*

In the corner he saw Bugsy and Floyd, in their usual spot. He didn't know whether he was relieved or disappointed. If they hadn't been there, he would have at least been forced to face himself alone with his thoughts about Elizabeth. But this way he knew that he could retreat behind the wall of Bugsy-and-Floyd-ishness, the same wall he had used to lie to Elizabeth earlier. God, he had to cool it with that kind of stuff. If only he hadn't felt so *desperate*. How did you not feel like you were born to run when you were with a girl? He was sure Bugsy and Floyd weren't going to be able to help him out on this score.

Sam walked up to his friends. "Hey," he said, plopping his knapsack on the table and taking a seat. He put his head in his hands momentarily.

"Hey, guy," Floyd said, slapping him on the back so heartily that Sam jerked up. "It won't be that bad. Bugsy here's got a whole study scheme worked out: flash cards, mnemonics, everything."

"Oh, yeah?" Sam said, adding silently, *Can he make one up for Elizabeth Wakefield?*

Chapter Eight

Well, it's lucky both my lovely sister and my best friend, Nina, could be there for me in the midst of my confusion, thought Elizabeth sarcastically as she walked through the quad toward SVU's library, looking grumpily at all the clumps of happy students splayed out all over the campus, leaning over their books and gossiping with friends. What was it lately with her group of friends anyway? First she'd thought she'd never stop arguing with Sam. Then, the minute things were going well with him, both Jessica and Nina decided to start acting like Marge's two older sisters on *The Simpsons*. Well, maybe there was a quota for people not getting along once spring fever hit or something.

Elizabeth passed a wall papered with posters for the dance, all of them with a shot of Leonardo DiCaprio on the prow of the *Titanic*. *I'm King of the Dance Floor!* was in huge, bold typeface below his cute mug. Maybe someone should tell the semiformal committee's advertising department that the whole Leo-*Titanic* thing was sort of old at this point.

Omigod, the *semiformal*. She would have to get a dress. Sam *would* think to get a tux, right? She wouldn't float downstairs in her dance attire to find him waiting there in his jeans and black T-shirt, would she?

An echo of Nina's "he should be sweating *your* feelings, girl," passed through Elizabeth's mind, but she dismissed it just as quickly. Sam just wasn't *like* that. You would have to be a zombie not to be empathetic about the fact that after his disastrous relationship with his parents, he was jumpy about close ties.

Elizabeth pushed through the library's revolving doors and headed to the back of the first floor, where she knew there'd be some empty seats at tables. No one liked to hang on the first floor for some unknown reason.

The section was absolutely mobbed—students who probably hadn't hit the library since their freshman-year tours were hunched over tables with huge stacks of books beside them, their hair greasy and unkempt from days without showering.

Well, I look like I've just come from the VH-1

Fashion Awards compared to everyone here, Elizabeth thought with some amusement. For a girl who normally dressed like a cross between Mia Hamm and Martha Stewart, donning Jessica's pink minidress, strappy sandals, and sorority-girl makeup that morning had felt as radical as putting on a three-foot tiara and an ermine robe.

"Whoa," exhaled a surfer-type dude with a shock of incredibly white blond hair as Elizabeth plopped her books across from him.

"Do you mind if I sit here?" she asked crisply, trying to keep any hint of a flirt out of her voice. It was interesting that she was attracting a totally different type of guy geared up this way, but she had enough problems right now.

"I don't mind *anything* you do," the guy said, talking as if he had a Hacky Sack kicking around somewhere within his throat. Elizabeth rolled her eyes and opened her journalism book, trying to concentrate.

Her e-mail! She would check her e-mail. Maybe Sam had sent a nice letter or something. *Well, that was all of three seconds you spent studying, Liz,* she congratulated herself.

Elizabeth grabbed her wallet and headed over to the network of terminals on a lower floor. There was a small line, but a short little guy in glasses near the front waved Elizabeth ahead of him. She didn't want to irritate everyone else, but she was kind of pressed for time. *Is this how Jessica lives every day?* she wondered, smiling at the guy, taking a seat, and typing in her password.

Nada. Well, if he was with Bugsy and Floyd, he was probably sitting in front of some huge coffee-stirrer tower Bugsy had constructed, arguing the relative merits of *The Matrix* versus *The Devil's Advocate* while Floyd tried fruitlessly to hold up flash cards and get them to study. Elizabeth smiled despite herself. Why couldn't Jessica and Nina see the good parts in Sam? Getting angry, Elizabeth began to think that she couldn't see how they *avoided* seeing Sam's virtues; they were so clearly there. Like, look at Finn. Sam had been so supportive of her during the Finn debacle, and he was the one that had known—and warned Elizabeth—that Finn was a jerk, right from the beginning.

Thank God I didn't lose my virginity to Finn, Elizabeth thought for the seven-hundredth time. Sam—Sam was someone she could see losing her virginity to for real. Sam would never mock or pressure her like Finn had. And he would also never sleep with Elizabeth just to get a notch in his belt—Sam was much more likely to run away when she brought up the subject than to whip out his ten pack of Trojan condoms.

107

Elizabeth stood up from the computer, groaning with irritation that she had so much studying to do when all she wanted to do was think about Sam. As she made her way out of the computer room, she caught a flash of blond in the corner of her eye that looked Jessica-esque. She sneaked around a pillar for a closer look.

It *was* Jessica, looking like she'd eaten a handful of nails for breakfast. Well, finals were enough to kill anyone's buzz. Still, Elizabeth had had enough of *Are you crazy?* for today, thank you very much. She sneaked back to her table with Mr. Baywatch Jr., trying to plot out the best route to avoid Jessica while leaving the library.

"Wow, man, there are, like, two of you," the guy gushed, having clearly spotted Jessica.

"Yup," said Elizabeth, hefting her backpack over her shoulder. She walked around three large bookcases, then skipped out past the guard without showing the inside of her backpack so that Jessica wouldn't see her standing in full view of the entire library. *And three's a crowd.*

Neil shoved his wallet into his back pocket, wildly trying to arrange his folder with Mona's number written on the front with a huge handful of change while he dialed the number of the phone company, hoping not to drop everything on the floor in front of everyone in the student center. He had abandoned the house not long after Jessica left, fearing that the minute he called anyone, Elizabeth or Sam would put in an appearance, and he would be forced to make the announcement that he was moving out before he had even settled things on his end.

"Please deposit three dollars and twenty-five cents," the mechanized voice on the phone informed him. What? This was a local call. Neil hung up and dialed again. *"Please deposit seventy-five cents,"* the voice said. That was better. He plopped in three quarters and sighed while the phone dialed.

The student center was surprisingly quiet today, given that it was finals week. Students sat silently at round plastic tables or on couches, hunched over their books, sipping coffee and chewing gum quietly. It was very different from the frantic atmosphere of the library, where you could practically *see* the electric fields of tension zigzagging out from each student. Here the entire phone bank had been empty rather than crowded with students frantically calling distant relatives to ask them to explain some weird area of physics or why James Madison had been sent over to France to handle the Louisiana Purchase.

Neil eased over a plastic chair with his left

foot so that he could sit while he was put on hold. A series of ads for various phone-company services streamed through his ear—no Muzak anymore? It was just talking, talking, talking. He eased the phone down to his cheek so he could hear when the voice changed to a real person but not feel it blasting through his ears at eighty-seven decibels. Well, this was what his life would be like from now on—a monastic retreat from all the hecticness of the twenty-first century. Neil smiled to himself. Had that been a weaving loom he had seen in the corner of Mona's bedroom or some other kind of crafty contraption? He wouldn't be surprised. Mona was so *natural,* she probably pulled her water from a well and made her own paper too.

A human voice finally came on. "I'm interested in getting my own phone line," Neil said hurriedly, reading off the new address for the woman. "And I would like my name taken off *this* address." Neil gave her his old information.

"You'll have to get a signed letter and a copy of your new lease for that," the woman said.

Neil was totally taken aback. "Get everyone to sign?" he said. "I thought I could just switch."

"If it's a single-person home, as a courtesy we allow customers to retain their old numbers when they switch," explained the woman. "But if you're leaving a group line for a new line, you must pay both a cutoff fee and a start fee."

"How much is that?" Neil said. After Mona cashed her check, he quickly calculated, he'd have about fifty-seven dollars in his checking account. That should be enough to cover this type of thing.

"The cutoff fee is seventy-five dollars, which can be waived if we're not interrupting service to the existing line, which will apply only after we receive the signed copy of your new lease. The start-up fee is eighty dollars, which we can break up over a series of quarterly payments if you like. Also, unless your new home already has two lines, there will be an additional installation fee of ninety-nine dollars, which we can break up over a year into four payments of twenty-five dollars. . . ."

Neil had stopped listening after "the cutoff fee is seventy-five." God, where was he going to get that kind of money? He would have to add some hours onto his part-time job in the dean's office. Maybe even get a credit card and rack it up, something he had avoided doing ever since he'd witnessed the kind of debt troubles his fellow students could get into. Whatever it was, it was going to take some serious maneuvering on his part and maybe even some sacrifice.

But sacrifice in a quiet place, he reminded himself.

*　　　*　　　*

Todd jerked his head up out of its nest of pillows, feeling like a series of jackhammers were going to work on his brain. God, what time was it? He'd only meant to go down for a quick nap after he'd found out Sweet Valley's major corporations weren't so sweet on college dropouts. He had been going to do something. . . . What was he going to do? Oh, call other companies and find out their policies on "independents," as he'd decided to call himself, before the working day was out. He knocked some newspapers off the overturned plastic crate he used as a bedside table to get a look at the clock. Four o'clock—only one hour left to get to work. Well, that just about killed that plan.

Todd stumbled to his feet, rubbing his face and shoulders to try to get some of the kinks out. He staggered into the bathroom to splash some water on his face. Looking up into his cracked, yellowy mirror, he noticed some new lines on his forehead and around his eyes. He peered closer. Nah. Those must just be from oversleeping today or something. And those bags too.

Kicking his Sony Playstation out of the way, Todd settled down on his living-room couch with the phone book. During his job search he'd circled all possible companies and stuck a Post-it on each relevant page. Efficient, huh? He was going to call them all again, even those he'd eliminated for being too small, too wacky, or too . . . something. Now wasn't a time to get picky.

"Please, please still be there," Todd muttered to himself as he dialed the first number. He went through the obligatory series of computerized questions, got a receptionist, and asked for human resources. He was transferred immediately.

"May I speak to the head of human resources, please?" Todd asked politely.

"Mr. Gilpin's not in. May I take a message?" the receptionist asked.

"Um . . . I'm calling to find out opportunities for . . . um . . . independents at . . . um . . . Grayscale, Inc.," he said, hurriedly sneaking a glance down at the phone book.

Silence. "Independent voters?" the receptionist finally asked.

Todd mentally kicked himself. "No . . . uh . . . I mean . . . freelancers, I guess," he said, locating the word with great relief.

"What type of freelance work do you do?" the receptionist asked.

"I'm an independent business consultant," Todd said firmly.

"Oh," said the receptionist. "Grayscale retains an independent consulting firm at this time. But if you'd like to send in your résumé, we'll make sure that it's sent to the appropriate department."

Yeah, the Department of Garbage Cans, Todd thought. He hurriedly interrupted him before he was cut off. "May I ask one more question?" he said.

"Certainly," the receptionist responded. Todd pictured him: young, in a sleek gray suit, probably glancing at his watch at this very moment.

"What's your policy on . . . um . . . college graduates?" Todd asked.

"We like 'em," the receptionist responded, putting on a faux-western twang. Ha ha.

Todd laughed nervously. "But . . . I mean . . . what if someone isn't a college student or doesn't have a college degree?" he said.

The receptionist suddenly sounded much less friendly and much more anxious to move things along. "Grayscale requires all of its *professional*-level employees to have a college degree," he said. "Nonprofessionals aren't required to have degrees. Does that answer your question?"

"I guess," said Todd. But wait. Maybe the *non*professional-level employees were really cool: independent consultants, creative designers, project ringers, that type of thing. "What exactly do you mean by nonprofessional?"

The receptionist had switched from a little bored to a little sympathetic, but he still sounded like he would be very, very pleased to get off the phone. "You know . . . mail room, janitorial, cafeteria. That kind of thing," he said. "Does that answer your question?"

Todd was too stunned to speak. He had really, really been living in dreamland, he could now see. "Um . . . yeah," he said. "Thanks."

"Have a nice day," the guy signed off cheerfully. Sure. A nice day and a nice life working at Frankie's . . . forever.

Todd looked at the clock again. Jeez! It was a quarter of five *already*. He threw on a baseball cap, catapulted himself down the stairs, and jumped onto his rickety bike, wincing as he tried to get his still stiff muscles used to the idea of pedaling again. Well, if he hadn't appreciated the glories of his BMW before, he'd certainly be able to if he had it now. His weekends too, which were lost in a haze of work and partying—with his coworkers. Ever since he'd started working full-time at Frankie's, his coworkers were the people he hung with all day. So it made sense that they'd become his circle of friends.

Weird. Coming home at 5 A.M., sleeping all day, then leaving again—this certainly wasn't the life of independence and leisure he had planned when he'd dropped out of college to become an "independent." Freelancer. Whatever.

Assistant manager, he reminded himself. Of a bar. Not that there was anything wrong with that. He saw himself at Sweet Valley High School's five-year reunion, wearing a name tag. *Hi. I'm Todd Wilkins, college dropout and assistant manager at Frankie's. I get to open and close the bar, I get to know the secret password to the safe, and I get to make three bucks more an hour than the back-bar guy I used to be before my promotion! If it's really busy at the bar, I might even find myself helping out by slicing limes. Whoo-hoo! I'm so impressive!*

He didn't like the sound of that at all.

Jessica could have sworn it was her Sam-obsessed sister that she'd just seen, ducking out of the main doors of the library like she was trying to avoid her or something. Well, she probably was, Jessica realized. First Neil, then Elizabeth—were her parents going to start refusing her calls? In the middle of a horde of study-hungry students Jessica was surprised to feel tears start to prick up in her eyes. *Jessica, please do not cry,* she hissed at herself. *That will be the final humiliation on a not-very-perfect day already, okay?*

Jessica took a deep breath and regained her composure, staring down at her art book as if it were the new J. Crew catalog to calm her thoughts. *Hmmm, that's nice,* she thought, looking at the cute hats and sundresses.

It was hopeless. She wanted to cry, and she knew exactly what the problem was: It had been ages since she and her sister had hung out. When they'd first come to college, it had been a lot like high school. Both of them had had their own sets of friends, of course (Elizabeth still retained her old taste for the dullest, nerdiest folks she could lay her hands on), but they'd still kept that old sister thing going: borrowing each other's clothes, talking constantly, acting like they still lived across the hall from each other, as they did at home.

Now that they *did* live across the hall from each other again (well, they were separated by a flight of stairs), they'd never been farther apart. Elizabeth was off every five seconds of the day studying something and throwing herself at some loser like Finn or Sam, and Jessica was . . . well, what was Miss Jessica doing? Yelling about everyone's love life to everyone, like Neil. Neil wasn't exactly Mr. Gossip, so he probably didn't appreciate Jessica's tirade. Especially not during finals week.

Maybe I'm so obsessed with my sister's love life because my own sucks, Jessica considered. *Nah. No way. Well, could be a little. But it's really because I actually love Elizabeth.* Not that that was such a revelation; it was more that Jessica hadn't put much energy into worrying about other people before. *Maybe I have grown up this year. Maybe I have changed into the more mature, more serious girl I wanted to be when sophomore year started.* Freaky.

I have not been a full member of life lately, Jessica thought glumly. *I don't know if Life would even recognize me if I showed up at his door.*

Before she could stop it, a tear ran off the edge of her nose and dropped onto van Gogh's *Starry Night. Perfect,* Jessica thought, stroking the spine of the book. *This book only cost nine thousand dollars or something.*

Wait. What was the name of the place where she had bought this book when the school's bookstore had run out? It was a gallery that showcased local Sweet Valley artists, connected to a small bookstore and museum-type shop that served cappuccinos and Belgian pastry.

She couldn't remember the name of the place, but she'd find it on the receipt. The gallery was in a kind of industrial district, and after Jessica had gotten the book (she had found it immediately; they had an excellent collection for such a tiny place), she had sat outside in the sun, drinking an espresso at one of the wrought-iron tables. There had totally been a bunch of arty-type people hanging out there: not only students with those lunch-box-type cases for their pastels, but older people with silk suits and interesting glasses—clearly other artists and dealers who lived in the area.

Jessica hadn't stayed long because she'd had to go to a Theta meeting. But that place had been totally cool and totally off the beaten path of the typical Sweet Valley student. What if she tried to get a summer internship there? Would they be interested in someone who was majoring in art history? Or would you have to be an artist or something? Jessica wasn't totally sure if she wanted to continue majoring in art history, but working at a gallery would be so awesome. If she could get hired.

I'm a fast learner, Jessica thought. Even though Professor Greenfield scared her to death, she'd done really well on her first two papers. Even the final might not turn out to be a disaster if Professor Greenfield overlooked the fact that she had a schizophrenic student. Jessica bet that Professor Greenfield knew the owner of the gallery and could write her a recommendation if she felt like it. Doing something in her own life—and having time to go on dates with guys like Clyde and Brett instead of worrying about who Elizabeth was dating—might be exactly what she needed to get her out of this train-wreck-of-a-life moment.

Totally reinvigorated by the idea of becoming a glamorous gallery assistant—Jessica had already begun to picture the black, heavy glasses and gray cashmere turtlenecks she was going to have to buy—Jessica slammed her book shut and stood up. Enough studying.

She was going to run out to the video store, get some munchies and stuff, and hog-tie Neil and Elizabeth to the couch. The three of them were going to hang out, like it or not. She was also going to find her old résumé on her hard drive and write a very, very nice note to Professor Greenfield, asking if she could be of any help in finding a summer internship at a gallery.

Jessica Wakefield had grown up, and everyone better love it—or leave it.

Chapter
Nine

Chloe stood in front of the library, tapping her foot. This was totally *the* spot to meet hotties during finals—had that been the entire swim team that just walked by? Chloe wasn't sure. But what she had noticed—right away—was that guys were finally, at long last, looking *her* over instead of looking right through her.

Chloe coughed, hoping that it would draw the attention of a particularly snackable upperclassman who was trying to fix a broken backpack strap before he went inside. He glanced up but looked right down again when he saw that no one was dying of whooping cough. Or at least, Chloe thought he had looked up. She was trying to cultivate a distant gaze, looking off toward the other side of campus as if she were waiting for a friend.

"Do you have the time?" a male voice queried.

Chloe looked up. A different guy—not the snackable one, but this one was okay—was standing in front of her, flexing his toes and arching his eyebrows. Here he was! It had happened finally—a public pickup. Chloe was *sure* he wanted more than the time.

"It's . . . um . . . four-thirty," she said, scrutinizing her watch as if the numerals were appearing in alien code.

"Thanks," the guy said briskly, running to catch up with his friend, who was holding the door. His very pretty friend, Chloe noticed.

Okay, so he was taken, Chloe coached herself. *But he was totally into you, I'm sure. Why else would he ask you for the time and not anyone else? Stretch much, Chlo?*

Chloe looked around. Of course, there was no one on the steps . . . right now. But there probably had been others, with watches, a minute before.

Chloe unfolded the *Allure* magazine she had brought with her for company and took a seat on the concrete railing. This position would show off her legs particularly well, she thought. She was just getting into an article on the proper method for preparing your feet for a pedicure when a shadow fell across the page.

"Hey, sexpot," a voice said. A female voice.

Chloe glanced up to find Nina looking down at her, amused.

"Hi," Chloe said, finding herself absurdly pleased that someone she knew was there to check out her new look. She jumped off the railing and twirled around. "Whaddya think?"

Nina was silent for a second, hitching her backpack up again on both shoulders. "Well," she said finally, "it's definitely . . . a *change*."

Chloe pushed her sunglasses up on her forehead so she could look Nina directly in the eyes. Nina couldn't be dissing her now, could she? If she was, it must be because she was jealous. "But a change for the better, don't you think?" she asked anxiously.

Nina folded her arms across her chest and eyeballed Chloe as if she were trying to classify a bug under a microscope. She sighed. "All right, I'll be honest," she said, furrowing her brow. "It's kind of over the top, don't you think?"

Chloe wanted to stamp her foot. "But *you* dress this way," she practically hissed.

Nina sighed. "Yeah," she said. "But Chloe, you have such an . . . I don't know exactly how to say it . . . *innocent* beauty, you know?"

Chloe was smoldering. "So you're saying I look like a girl dressing up in her sophisticated older sister's clothes," she said.

"Well," Nina said, laying her hand on Chloe's arm, "a little. Don't you?"

Jealous! Chloe wanted to spit, shaking off Nina's

hand. "No, I do not. I think I look hot," she said.

Nina sighed again. "Of course you do, Chloe. But don't you want a guy to like you for more than your bod?" she asked.

I just want a guy to like me, period! Chloe wanted to scream. She huffily put on her sunglasses and sat back down. "That's not really the point," she said.

Nina looked at her watch. "I better go," she said. "Good luck, okay? Tell me what happens."

Yeah, right, Chloe thought. "Okay," she said sullenly. She could not *believe* Nina had just done that to her on her maiden voyage as a hot babe. What was she, a grandmother in training?

"Hey, do you have the time?" a voice said.

Not again. Chloe looked at her watch and back down at the *Allure*. "Four forty-five," she muttered.

She felt someone sit down next to her. A match flickered, and Chloe looked up, face-to-face with a dead ringer for Ryan Phillippe. Ryan clone squinted and exhaled a plume of smoke.

"What's your name?" he asked Chloe.

Chloe had to steel herself to not look around to make sure he wasn't talking to somebody else. "Chloe. You?" she said, trying to appear both unimpressed and seductive at the same time.

"James," he said, sticking out his hand. "You look like you're working really hard," he added.

God, not two people harshing on her in five minutes! Chloe was about to stand up and tell him off when she realized he was talking about the *Allure,* not *her* allure. Jeez. She wasn't sure if her ego could have stood it. But this guy, thankfully, was definitely flirting with her.

"Well, I have a test on pedicures on Monday," Chloe joked, sticking out her foot.

"Do you think you'd have time to have a cappuccino or something before then?" James asked, standing up and sticking his pack of cigarettes in his front pocket. He'd said it with a totally blank face, as if he were asking about the weather.

"S-Sure!" Chloe stuttered. Too eager. "I think," she added.

James threw his messenger bag over his shoulder. "How about eight tonight?" he asked, his hands in his pockets.

"Um . . . okay," Chloe said. This was happening so fast. How did Nina and Jessica handle it all the time? She loved it, though—she felt like she could talk to James, while he squinted at her and smiled, forever.

"'Kay. How about Yum-Yums? A back table. Be there," James said with a smile as he pointed at her and wheeled off.

Chloe was panting a little. "Oh, I'll be there."

She wanted to break out in the Mariah Carey version, she was so beyond happy. "I'll be there!"

Elizabeth ran up the library steps, afraid to check behind her to find out if her sister had seen her bolt from the library like Harrison Ford in *The Fugitive*. This relationship with Sam—all twenty hours of it, or whatever it had been—was becoming exactly the pain in the neck she didn't need right now. Unfortunately, most of the bad part of it was coming from Jessica and Nina—the two people she had expected to remain levelheaded while Sam went completely out of his gourd.

Elizabeth stopped in the middle of the quad and looked around her, taking a deep breath. The sun was just beginning to set, and students were headed back to their dorms and apartments in twos and threes in the lengthening shadows. Elizabeth dragged the edge of her notebook along the side of a wall. This time of year—the end of spring, just before everyone would go away for the summer—always made her especially wistful, although she didn't know why. It must be the combination of everything ending and beginning at the same time. Finals . . . and Sam.

Just thinking of Sam flooded Elizabeth with such a warm, goofy feeling that she was forced to stop for a second and grin. A gaggle of ponytailed girls swinging their lacrosse sticks passed her. Sam. Sam. Sam. Sam. She couldn't wait to see him again. Couldn't wait to spend a romantic evening with him, even if all they did was hang out in his room and listen to music.

Elizabeth stopped in her tracks again. A candle-light dinner! That was exactly what she and Sam needed to mark this period, something that would take them from the end of the year into the summer. *That's* why she usually got sad—people left relationships hanging at the end of the year, things went unsaid, and connections got lost in the wake of finals and good-byes. But she wasn't going to let that happen to her and Sam: They would have a dinner at the house, talk over their expectations, and be able to go to the semiformal without feeling worried that the night was either the end of everything or the beginning of nothing.

She hadn't yet made summer plans. And if Sam had any, he hadn't mentioned them. Wouldn't it be great if they both decided to stay at the house and get mindless summer jobs?

Elizabeth began walking quickly toward town, biting her lips and planning a menu in her head. Steaks? Nah. Too much sawing back and forth and too much money, usually. What about flan for dessert? Normally she was a good cook, but the last time she had tried to make flan, she had wound up with a yellow goop that looked like vanilla pudding and tasted like scrambled egg yolks. Chocolate mousse was easier and safer—she could do it first and put it in the refrigerator to chill. . . .

Elizabeth headed into Del Banco's, the incredibly expensive and fancy gourmet grocery where she allowed herself to shop only for special occasions. Opening the screen door, she breathed in the scent of fresh herbs, cheese, and just baked bread. *It's a shame they don't have a meal plan,* she thought, sniffing some sprigs of rosemary and popping a crumbled piece of Gruyère into her mouth. Del Banco's was famous for its samples—some students allegedly weren't allowed inside on Sunday mornings anymore, having helped themselves to entire plates of bruschetta and cream-cheese brownies instead of sticking to the toothpicked itty-bitty bites the owner laid out diligently.

Wanting to shove handfuls of jars of olives and sun-dried tomatoes into her cart, Elizabeth tried to concentrate. First things first. She headed over to the fish counter, finally deciding on a pair of fresh salmon steaks, which the man behind the counter wrapped and marked with his Magic Marker. Now, what would go well with salmon? Not the Chinese vegetables she usually threw together for stir-fry. Her eye fell on the bundles of fresh asparagus stacked by the register. Perfect.

Now some bitter chocolate, some heavy cream, some little mushrooms for rice pilaf, and she would be finished.

Her cart brimming with the perfect evening, Elizabeth began laying out her stuff on the counter for the woman behind the register. $78.60! *Well, there goes my budget for the month,* Elizabeth thought, handing over her rarely used credit card and wincing slightly. But it was worth it. It was an investment in her future—hers and Sam's. She gathered up her bags and walked out into the dusk. *We're worth it.*

Jessica hummed to herself on the way back from the video store, totally caught up in her fantasies of being a prima gallerina. She had gotten *My Best Friend's Wedding* and *Wild Things* off the racks, the first to placate her sister, who had a total crush on Rupert Everett, and the second for Neil, who had said publicly that he would run naked through the quad during exams for five minutes in Matt Dillon's presence.

She had also stopped by a small jewelry store next door to Blockbuster, totally on impulse. In the window there had been a small, silver frame with a filigree around the edges. The placement picture inside was of two blond twin girls, one grinning wickedly, the other smiling happily. The moment Jessica saw it, she knew she'd have to give it to Elizabeth, maybe as an early birthday present. That, even more than the Chee•tos and the videos, was going to give her the message that family was there for you forever, whereas liar boyfriends weren't.

"Hel-looooo," Jessica called, swinging into the kitchen. Something smelled *amazing*. What was that—dill? And chocolate something? And sautéed mushrooms?

Elizabeth was standing at the table, chopping like a madwoman. A mixing bowl that had clearly held some delectable chocolate mixture was in the sink, along with other assorted pots and pans. The rice cooker was steaming, and her sister was whipping something delicious looking up with heavy cream and dill. In front of Elizabeth, Jessica saw salmon steaks: two. Meaning one for Sam. Jessica felt a black cloud of fury settle over her head. So much for sisters' night at home.

"Oh, Liz—how nice of you to go to all this trouble for me," Jessica said coldly.

Elizabeth looked up, her eyes narrowed.

Before Elizabeth could say anything, Jessica cut her off. "Don't worry—I was just kidding." She placed the bag of videos and junk food on the table.

"Pass me the colander," Elizabeth said, again focusing on her cooking.

Jessica wordlessly handed over the bowl, crossing her arms over her chest. "Well, this is great," she finally said.

Elizabeth sighed, then dumped a handful of chopped dill into the bowl and mixed it ferociously. "What's great? And I do assume you're being sarcastic."

"That you're going to fail all your finals." Jessica leaned over her sister's shoulder, peered into the many plates and bowls lining the counter, then scooped up a fingerful of chocolate whip. "Mmmm," she said. "Mousse."

Elizabeth pushed the bowl out of Jessica's reach. "Why am I going to fail all my finals?"

"Because you're majoring in *Sam,* that's why," Jessica sniped.

Elizabeth rolled her eyes, then bent down to put the salmon steaks in the oven. She turned around to face Jessica. "I think you're forgetting that I'm a straight-A student. And you're really one to talk, Jess. The minute you have a boyfriend, you forget everything else."

Jessica toyed with the ends of her hair. Okay, so Elizabeth had a point on that one.

Elizabeth eyed her sister. "What's it to you, Jess? I want the truth. Why are you suddenly Ms. Concerned all of a sudden?"

Jessica stopped for a second. It was a reasonable

question. She wasn't exactly famous for her concern for others, even her own sister. She stared at the floor, stumped. *What is it to me?* she wondered.

"I think I know."

Jessica and Elizabeth swiveled to face Neil, standing in the doorway.

He ran a hand through his silky dark hair, his gray eyes focused on Jessica. "I think you're so against your sister and Sam as a couple because it makes her human."

"Oh, so I was an alien before?" Elizabeth asked.

Neil smiled. "I just mean that Jess has always looked up to you as the twin who always does the right thing. You think before you act."

"So?" Jessica said. "That's nothing new."

"Right," Neil agreed. "But now Elizabeth is following her heart. Her head might be telling her that Sam's a risk as a boyfriend. But her heart is obviously telling her to go for it."

"Omigod, Neil, that's exactly how I feel," Elizabeth exclaimed.

"Wait, so what does this have to do with me?" Jessica asked.

Neil walked to the counter, eyed the goods, and stuck a pinkie in the chocolate whip. He licked his lips. "Well, I think that you're discovering that Lizzie here is human like everyone else.

She fell in love with a challenging guy—a great guy, but not your average idiot. So I think you"— he pointed at Jessica—"are worried that you're losing the sister who's always driven you crazy but who you like just the way she is—was."

"Did you just take your psych final or something?" Jessica asked, looking confused.

Elizabeth laughed. "I think I know what Neil means. You're afraid if *I* fall in love and go off the deep end, like by cooking up an expensive storm during finals week, that the rest of you don't have much hope."

Neil nodded. "Exactly."

"Some of what you said sounds right," Jessica said. "But what I'm really worried about is Elizabeth getting hurt."

"So tell her, not me," Neil said with a smile, and left the kitchen.

Jessica picked up the bag of videos and dumped them out, rattled the bags of Chee•tos and M&M's, then slapped the wrapped frame onto the table. "I know I've been on your case lately, so I got this stuff for a cheesy sisters' night."

Elizabeth picked up the present, looked at Jessica, then slowly unwrapped it. When she saw the frame and the picture, tears welled up in her eyes. Jessica tried to stop the tears stinging the backs of her own eyes, but she couldn't. "Oh, Jessica. I'm sorry." She pulled Jessica into a hug, and they both started sobbing together.

"No, I'm sorry," Jessica said. "I've been a total shrew. I don't know what's wrong with me."

Elizabeth pulled back from Jessica and looked her in the eyes. "Jessica, you know that this thing with Sam and me isn't going to cut away from our relationship. It's just the beginning, and I—"

Jessica was sniffling. Maybe she'd been freaking out because of *everything*. Elizabeth, finals, Neil not being around so much, her Theta friends getting annoyed that she wasn't concentrating on the sorority enough. "No, I understand." *I mean, c'mon, I cast a wide net when I date, don't I?* she thought. Maybe her sister should have the same privilege. Anyway, she was going to have an entirely new career at a gallery in the next week or two, and all of this would bother her a lot less. "Really. I do."

Elizabeth looked at her, trying to sort out if Jessica was being accommodating, not a mode she generally entered. "Really?" she asked.

Jessica gave one last sniffle, hoping this crying jag hadn't totally made her look like a pink sewer rat. "Really."

Elizabeth grinned widely. "Good," she said, giving her sister a quick kiss on the cheek. "Because I have to get back to cooking."

That comment almost sent Jessica through the roof again, but she controlled herself. "Great," she said, offering up a big, forced smile. She picked up the bag of videos and moved to the living room, turning on the TV and flipping channels until she found E! She burrowed down into the sofa cushions, watching Joan and Melissa Rivers deconstruct some actress's terrible clothing choices.

I guess the Sam era has begun, Jessica thought. *Time to ring it in with Neil. Where'd that boy go anyway?*

Elizabeth wiped a garlicky-smelling hand on her nose, trying to scratch an itch while mixing up dill sauce at the same time. She looked at the clock: Should she start to steam the asparagus now or wait until Sam got home? *Just wait,* she cautioned herself. There was nothing more disgusting than limp, colorless asparagus.

That had been a very, very close escape with Jessica. Her sister was prone to drama, but this had been a little over the top even for her. Still, the frame was very beautiful, and it was true that she and Jessica hadn't been close this semester. Elizabeth looked at the frame, which she'd placed on the counter—she'd have to dig around for a real picture of her and Jessica to fill it.

Sam would be home soon. Elizabeth's stomach

gave a quick flip at the thought. It would be so amazing, just the two of them, alone for the evening in his room. And who knew what would happen afterward . . .

Don't get ahead of yourself, she cautioned herself. She had to keep reminding herself that this whole thing had only started last night, not last year. Still, her feelings for Sam were so strong that they overrode every cautious bone in her body—and she had a lot of them.

Elizabeth gave the rice a quick stir, checked on the salmon, and went down to the basement to find the old card table she knew was hanging around. Lugging it up from downstairs, she plopped it in the middle of Sam's room, wiped all the dust off with an old rag, and covered it with a linen tablecloth Mrs. Wakefield had given the girls when they'd gone off to college. After she'd set it, lit two candles, and arranged some gladiola blossoms from the yard floating open in a bowl, she sat back and surveyed the scene.

This better not scare the hell out of Sam, Elizabeth thought, gnawing that lower lip like crazy.

Chapter Ten

Sam had stopped off on his way home to buy some flowers for Elizabeth. He thought it would be a nice gesture, considering the fact that he had totally blown her off earlier in the day.

The florist had arranged a small bouquet of lilies, roses, and some stuff Sam had never even heard of. The whole thing had cost thirty-eight dollars. Thirty-eight dollars! He'd had no idea flowers could be that expensive. That was, like, *three* CDs. Well, Bugsy and Floyd would have to spot him some cash this week, that was all. His housemates might think he had access to his family's fortune, but he didn't. Or more like he didn't allow himself access.

Sam put his face down in the bouquet and sniffed. The flowers reminded him of Elizabeth and what he loved about her: She was so elegant, classic, and amazing, yet she also was constantly surprising him with aspects of herself that he never could have predicted.

Wait, had he just said *love*? Sam stopped dead in his tracks on the quiet street, struck by how his thoughts had betrayed him.

He had always known that he was crazy about Elizabeth. But love was something else entirely. Love was freakin' *scary*.

He and Wakefield, in love? Did she feel that way about him? Was that really how he felt about her? Were the two of them about to fall in love? And was that even what he wanted?

Sam reached the house and pulled open the door, his stomach turning over uneasily. He hung up his coat, being careful not to crush the flowers, and walked into the kitchen.

He had hoped Elizabeth would be home, and she was—standing at the counter, cooking up a storm. *Argh*. Was all this for him? Sam didn't know how comfortable he felt about that. Having his dinner made for him instead of snarfing it out of some leftover box from Hunan Wok felt kind of . . . married.

Elizabeth looked up and smiled. At the sight of her smile Sam's toes curled. *See? It's easy. Just concentrate on how amazingly beautiful she is each time you get the jitters.*

"There's a surprise for you in your room," she said, looking sly.

Is it a one-way ticket to Mexico? Sam thought, then mentally berated himself for it. What kind of a guy was he that the sight of a beautiful girl cooking dinner made him want to flee the country? He tried to calm down.

"Oh, yeah?" he said, stepping forward with the flowers. "Well, these are for you."

Elizabeth dumped a handful of asparagus over a steaming grill and wiped her hands on her jeans. "Sam!" she exclaimed. "These are beautiful. I'm going to put them in water. Go to your room and see your surprise!" she ordered, rummaging around one of the higher cabinets for a vase.

"Okay, okay," Sam said, lifting his hands in mock surrender. He backed slowly out of the room and walked down the hall toward his door. He put his hand on the knob and opened it.

Gulp.

The candles, tablecloth, and flowers gently refracting off the china were supposed to be beautiful and sophisticated, but to him they looked totally cheesy and over the top. Buying flowers had been pushing the envelope; a candlelight dinner was totally in violation of his things-I-do-as-a-guy rules.

Sam broke out in a cold sweat. He wanted

Elizabeth—desperately—but at his speed, in his way. This type of thing—all of these arrangements, these public displays, these trips to Yum-Yums—was exactly the type of thing he was trying to avoid.

Sam realized that he was practically hyperventilating. He'd just started going out with Elizabeth, and he was already freaking. *Slow, man. Slow,* he cautioned himself. This didn't have to end in disaster, right?

He just didn't know how to stop it.

Sam looked around desperately, seeking an exit. But there was nowhere to go.

He was in *his* room.

Todd walked into Frankie's twenty minutes early, shaking off the light rain that had whipped up the minute he got on his bike. He was so stressed out, he had pounded his mountain bike's pedals like a triathlete and arrived there in half of his usual time.

His boss, Rita, who was on the phone, gave him a nod. He nodded back and headed into the back office, where he would sometimes read the paper on breaks or hang out after his shift. Today, however, his head felt so heavy that he couldn't keep it off the desk. A fifteen-minute snooze and he'd be raring to go. *Jeez,* he mumbled as he felt himself falling asleep. *I hope I don't drool all over Rita's papers.*

Suddenly Todd was standing at the bar handing out drinks. *Ah,* he realized. *I'm dreaming again.* But it wasn't the usual crowd of Frankie's regulars. Was that Jessica? And Elizabeth? And the three girls he'd been crushing on in his marketing class before he dropped out? There was Nina Harper too. And the guys he used to hang with his freshman year. Except they all looked grown-up, still young, but grown-up. Todd noticed that they were all wearing sophisticated business attire and carrying briefcases. They were chatting about an article they'd all read in *The Wall Street Journal.*

"Hey!" he called out. He tried to make his voice louder so they would hear him over the din. "Hey! It's me, Todd." They all squinted at him, as though trying to place him. "Todd Wilkins. From Sweet Valley."

Elizabeth tilted her head. "Oh my God! I never would have recognized you with your hair all long and wild."

"Yeah, and put on a few pounds there, bud?" asked a guy who Todd used to shoot hoops with. "I remember you from freshman year at SVU. You had washboard abs, man."

Dream Todd stared down at his gut. Okay, so he'd had one too many beers and too many problems with staffers to go work out at some fitness club.

Nina eyed him. "Did you read the article too, Todd?" She flickered softly in and out of focus. "Do assistant managers at bars read *The Wall Street Journal*?"

"I'm the *manager* now," Todd corrected. "I got promoted when Rita bought the place outright. I've been working here for five years now."

"You must have a fortune in stock options, then!" Jessica called out, then howled with laughter. Everyone joined in.

Elizabeth stared at him with pity in her eyes. She was shaking her head. "Do you guys remember when Todd and I were a major couple in high school?" she asked the group. "He was so different then!"

So different then . . . so different then . . . so different then . . .

"The service here is pathetic," one of the marketing girls said. "Hello! You, there—if you're *really* the manager, can we get a waitress or what?"

You there . . . you there . . . you there . . .

"It's me, Todd. Todd Wilkins," he told the girl, his voice laced with desperation. "Don't you remember me? I sat behind you in marketing sophomore year, well, before I dropped out. We worked on a project together. You flirted with me. . . . The name is Todd. Todd!"

"Todd! Todd! Todd!" kept ringing in his ears.

Somehow the voice penetrated the depths of his consciousness. "Todd! Todd! Back to earth, Todd!"

Todd's eyes opened, and he lifted his head. Rita was rapping him lightly on the head with a rolled-up newspaper. He'd been dreaming.

Relief flooded him. He stared at Rita, then grabbed her by the shoulders, grinning wildly. "It was just a dream! Just a terrible, horrible dream! A nightmare!"

Rita eyed him, smiling. "Yeah, and so's the fight between Annie and Monica over tables. Better get out there and break it up."

It was just a dream, he told himself again. It wasn't real.

But it *would* be. It would be if Todd kept on this path.

Suddenly it all hit him at once: his parents' anguish when he dropped out, the rejection letters for summer internships, the disdain in the human-resources woman's voice, all the girls who didn't have time to date him once he had dropped out of college.

Todd closed his eyes, counted to five, then opened them again. He had thought that dropping out of college was going to give him independence, some options above and beyond sitting in a lecture hall and burying himself in some carrel in the library. But now he saw the truth finally: He was a college dropout who broke up fights between drunken idiots, who sliced limes, who made sure there were enough bags of ice, who figured out the servers' schedules. There wasn't anything wrong with that job—once he'd been very proud of it. It was just that it wasn't what he wanted for life.

He'd wanted to be independent, to live like an adult instead of some rich college kid whose parents' credit card paid his way. But he'd been too stupid to realize that an *education* would give him *options*. And *options* equaled *independence*.

Todd felt like banging his head right on the counter of the bar.

"Rita," he said. "I've got an emergency. I need about two hours, then I'll be back. I'll make up the time tomorrow."

He saw the concern in Rita's warm brown eyes. "Something wrong?"

"Something has been wrong. But it won't be after today."

"Um, excuse me," Chloe said, pushing her way past a group of frat boys in front of Yum-Yums. *I've got a hot date, so get out of my way!* she added mentally.

"No, excuse *me,*" one of them said flirtatiously, executing a mock bow. He turned to the door and opened it with a flourish, extending his hand while the other held open the glass door. "This way, milady," he added in a fake English accent.

"Not at all," Chloe said, feeling like Audrey Hepburn in *Breakfast at Tiffany's.* She was beginning to get used to the attention-from-guys stuff. What in the world had Nina been talking about, with all of her warnings and frowns? That girl could be such a drag, really. Maybe Nina just hadn't learned to groove on her power yet, like Chloe had.

With a little secret thrill Chloe saw that James was already waiting for her at a back table, deeply absorbed in some book. As she approached the table, taking care not to trip and send some waitress flying, Chloe had to fight the urge to ask him to the semiformal right then and there.

"Hi," Chloe said, trying to utilize a soft, sultry voice that was a level or two deeper than her own.

James waited one split second before looking up. "Hey, there, sexy," he said, placing the book in his knapsack. He peered around the coffee lounge, signaled for a waitress, then leaned in conspiratorially to Chloe. "I have to confess something. I've been thinking about you ever since I met you." He sat back like he had just told Chloe he was the illegitimate son of Kurt Loder.

"But you just met me a couple of hours ago," Chloe said, biting back the words the minute they were out of her mouth. What was wrong with her? A guy started confessing his serious thing for her, and she knocked him right down.

"That's what I mean," said James, looking down and then up at her again and giving a half grin. "I haven't been able to stop thinking about you." He snaked one of his hands across the table, then covered Chloe's with it.

Chloe had to stop her inner self from getting up, cheering, and screaming, *Finally!* Her heart was totally palpitating, StairMaster style. God, satisfaction felt so great. She couldn't wait to see the faces of the Theta girls when she brought James over to the house.

The waitress came over, and Chloe could practically taste the scrumptious vanilla steamer she was about to order.

"We'll have two cappuccinos, very dry, please," James said quickly, "and some chocolate biscotti."

So much for the steamer. And what was a *dry* cappuccino? The waiter disappeared before Chloe could say she'd prefer something else. She glanced at James; he was looking at her with goo-goo eyes. *Do I want a vanilla steamer more than I want a date to the semiformal?* Chloe asked herself. *Uh, no!* So the guy was a little presumptuous and a teeny bit pretentious. No big deal. Maybe he thought ordering for a girl was chivalrous or something.

"So, um," Chloe started, then froze when she felt his hand suddenly stroke her thigh. *Ok-ay*, she thought. *A little quick. But he clearly likes you. Or your outfit. Either way, the new you is working.* "Do you like SVU?" *Oh, great question, Chloe,* she berated herself. *Really interesting way to start off a convo.*

"Who would?" he said. "SVU is *so* not cool. I'm only stuck here because my mother refuses to pay for me to go to school abroad and study art."

"Oh," Chloe said, glad when the cappuccinos arrived. She stirred hers wildly, hoping some of the foam would dissolve into the espresso, like whipped cream did. "What type of art are you interested in?"

Chloe had expected a really easy answer, like "modern art" or something. But instead James went into some really complicated answer that used words like *dada, Richter, photo-realism,* and *William Wegman.* "You know?" James finished, draining his glass and pushing the last of the two biscottis into his mouth. He hadn't even offered her one, Chloe noticed, before he'd inhaled them. Well, maybe he was really hungry or nervous.

Okay, so the guy wasn't her dream man. But he was cute, and he was here. That meant a potential dance date. He didn't have to turn into her boyfriend.

"So do you have your own room?" he asked her.

Now, this is more like it, Chloe thought happily, taking a sip of her practically undrinkable cappuccino. *He's asking questions, showing an interest in me, not just my thigh.* He'd removed his hand to eat and drink, but now it lay there again, heavy against the material.

"No," Chloe told him. "I wish, but I have a roommate. I live in Theta house." *That should score points,* she thought. Theta was the coolest sorority on campus.

James smiled. "So, whaddaya say we blow this joint and go hang at my apartment? I live off campus. It's kind of a walk, but we could, you know, get to know each other a little or something along the way." He stood up, left five bucks on the table, and pulled on his leather jacket.

Chloe stared at the money on the table. "Um, I think the bill is probably more than that. Capps are really expensive, and I think the biscotti is like two bucks each. I'll get it, though." Chloe pulled her wallet out of her knapsack.

"Thanks," he said. "That's cool of you. I'm running really low this week."

Hmmm, Chloe thought. *So far, everything is going really well. He thinks I'm an easygoing, cool girl, we're going to his place to listen to music or watch TV. . . . In an hour I should be able to brag up and down the quad about my hot date to the dance.*

Chloe followed James out of the café.

"Straight up this street for like half a mile, then we make a left, and we're there," James told her as he zipped his jacket. He waggled his eyebrows at her, and she laughed.

"So, what year are you?" Chloe asked, walking faster than she'd like in order to keep up with his pace. "I'm a freshman."

"I don't like labels," he replied. "Labels are a product of an oppressive society."

Huh, Chloe thought. *Is this guy a pretentious jerk or just a freshman like me who hates admitting he's the youngest year on the totem pole?*

"I totally understand," she said, and he smiled at her, a sexy, heart-stopping smile.

Finally they stopped in front of a battered metal door. James inserted a key, then led Chloe up a narrow, dark staircase. He glanced at her, then said, "It's not exactly luxury, but it's cheap, so . . ."

"I think it's really cool," she exclaimed, hoping she wasn't getting lead poisoning as they walked past another chipping wall. It was cute that he was embarrassed on her behalf.

James stopped in front of a red door, unlocked it, and ushered Chloe inside. "Home, sweet home," he said.

Chloe looked around in awe. The apartment was really cool. Not much furniture, except for a futon mattress, a coffee table made out of milk crates, and a bookcase. Posters and charcoal sketches covered every inch of the walls. And there were lots of books.

"It's just the one room," he said, "but I do have a separate kitchen." He gestured toward a doorway, and Chloe followed him into a tiny space with a half refrigerator and the smallest stove and sink she'd ever seen. "Can I offer you a drink?"

"Whatever you're having," she told him with a smile, then moved back into the main room. She sat down on the edge of the futon. *How cool is this?* she asked herself. *I decide to make something happen, and something happens. That is girl power!*

James walked into the room, holding two small glasses of a dark, oily liquid. He sat down beside her and handed her a glass. "My grandfather brought this back from a trip to Europe." James downed his in one gulp. He gestured toward Chloe's. "Try it."

Chloe sniffed the liquid. Pungent and sweet. She smiled at James, then took a delicate sip. *Yarg!* Her throat felt like she'd swallowed nail-polish remover.

"No, you have to do it all at once," James said with a grin as he moved closer to her. "Down it."

Chloe could feel his thigh against hers. "I want to make it last," she told him flirtatiously, hoping he didn't think she was unsophisticated. She placed the glass by her feet.

He snaked an arm around her shoulders, then began trailing gentle kisses down her cheek. "You have to lie back so I can kiss you properly."

Chloe leaned back on her elbows, then went fully back onto the futon. James had moved from her neck to her mouth and was hungrily kissing her. *Kinda fast again,* she thought. *Go with it, Chlo. He's hot, he's interesting (sort of), and he's into you. Just see where it goes.* She felt his hands inching up her stomach.

"Wait," Chloe said, sitting up very suddenly. "I don't even know your last name, James."

James rolled his eyes. "I thought I said labels weren't important to me." He leaned in again and began kissing her neck, his hands reaching under her skirt. *Whoa, there,* she thought. *Hold on a minute there, buddy. You're cute, but I'm not even really that attracted to you.*

"You're just moving kinda fast," she said, darting over a bit. "I *am* just a freshman," she added in her most adorable tone with a chuckle, but

James didn't seem to find that amusing.

"You're so pretty, I just can't resist you," he said, looking at her with a sweet expression. He pushed a strand of hair behind her ear, then lightly stroked her face. "I am so attracted to you." His hand clamped on her thigh, James moved closer to her, slowly pressing her down on the futon again so that he was lying on top of her. He began to inch his hands upward while he kissed her mouth so firmly, she could barely breathe, much less speak.

This was *so* not okay, Chloe thought angrily, hardly enjoying this burst of testosterone. How did you keep a guy under control when he got like this? Chloe had no idea. She tried pushing his hands away, but they just came back more insistently. Finally she forced herself upward again.

"What's wrong, Carrie?" he asked. "I thought you liked me."

That did it. Chloe snapped. What did James think—that she was going to sleep with him on the first *coffee*? He had another thing coming. She had to put her foot down.

"It's *Chloe*, not Carrie," she told him. "You're really close."

"Sorry," he mumbled. "I thought you said Carrie. So, c'mere. Why are you sitting way over there? I'm sorry." He eyed her with concern this time. "Like I said, I was just having trouble resisting you. You are so amazing looking. I could look into those blue eyes forever."

Chloe tried to remember the last time a guy had said that to her. She couldn't. It felt so good to be that girl for once, the girl who got guys all hot. But she wasn't looking to get all sexual with this guy. Once they went out a few times, then maybe. But Chloe was sort of inexperienced in the sex department. Very inexperienced. As in never had sex!

And she got the feeling James was expecting a lot tonight.

"I thought we'd hang out for a while," she told him, "you know, listen to music?"

He smiled, then put his arm around her, pulling her close to him. She didn't like that. He wasn't respecting anything about her. As the arm around her drew her even closer to him, so close, she was practically flattened uncomfortably against his chest, his other hand clamped on her thigh again, then started inching up, faster this time. "Oh, Chloe," he whispered. "You're so sexy. So hot. I want you so bad." The hand raced up her skirt.

Chloe tried to bat it away, but from her position against him, she couldn't. He deepened the kiss. Panic began to overtake Chloe; the cappuccino started sloshing in her stomach.

She tried to push him away. "Stop it, James," she ordered. "I'm serious. Stop it!"

"Come on," he whispered, "don't be like that."

As Chloe tried to wiggle out of his grasp, she suddenly saw the whole thing for what it was: James had only picked her up because she looked fun and easy, not because he was interested in her. He couldn't care less if her name was Chloe or Clorox. He was just in it for the miniskirt and eyeliner.

Chloe felt tears start in her eyes. *Think, girl,* she ordered herself. *Think and get out of here!* "Um, James, I think I'd relax if I had something else to drink, maybe some wine or beer?"

Chloe waited for him to take the bait. He did. He chuckled and whispered in her ear, "Good idea, baby. A little vino, and you'll be less nervous and feeling fine." He jumped up and headed into the kitchen.

Chloe took a fast, deep breath, then grabbed her knapsack and ran to the door, yanking it open and flying down the hall faster than she ever thought she could.

She'd run down the stairs and out the door and down the street before she took a breath. Only when she turned the corner and could see the familiar top part of Davis Hall looming ahead did she feel safe. She was back on her territory.

Tears streamed down Chloe's face. *I'm such an*

idiot, she told herself. *Such an idiot. He wasn't in-terested in you. He just wanted to have sex. You can't even interest a guy when you dress hot. Well, except in undressing you.*

Chloe caught a glimpse of herself in one of the closed-shop windows. She looked like an extra for a Marilyn Manson video, not a hot young babe just returning from a successful make-out session with a potential date for the biggest dance at SVU. *Get-*out session was more like it.

Where was she supposed to go now? She couldn't go back to Theta house; someone would ask what was wrong, and she'd make a fool out of herself by spilling her guts. And Val, who'd proba-bly be sympathetic but say *I told you so,* was surely out nerding around with Martin. She could always check in to the Sweet Valley Resort Hotel on her mom's credit card, but even a hot bubble bath in a luxury hot tub wouldn't soothe her. She needed someone to talk to.

Nina. Of course, Nina. Nina would help, and she'd probably be home too. And, Chloe thought ruefully, Nina would very likely be serving the house special: crow.

Elizabeth pulled the salmon out of the oven and put a cover on the bubbling rice and a cloth over the asparagus so that it wouldn't get limp while she went upstairs to freshen up. She fought the urge to run in and check on Sam's reaction to her lovely table setting for their intimate tête-à-tête. No. She wanted everything to be perfect when she walked in, not to peek in looking like she'd just emerged from a steam cooker herself.

Elizabeth ran upstairs to her room, kicked off her jeans, and took her still wet hair out of its ponytail holder (she had jumped in the shower just before she'd started cooking, knowing that Sam, as usual, would arrive unexpectedly). From her closet she took a white linen shift dress with an embroidered scoop neck, which she had been saving for an occasion exactly like this. Slipping on some simple Kenneth Cole slides, she ran a comb through her hair and fanned herself. A little Carmex and she was done. Hopefully Sam hadn't gotten too used to the glammed-up Elizabeth of this morning. If she took the time to put on all the makeup she'd worn earlier today, the salmon would taste like linoleum by the time she got downstairs.

She looked at herself in the small mirror that hung on the wall and frowned. Unfortunately, her hair looked like she'd ironed it with Crisco. Uh-oh. A little blow drying, clearly, would have to be in order.

She bopped into the bathroom, trying to keep

down her excitement about the fact that she and Sam were finally . . . an *item*. That she was going to spend the next half hour sitting across from him at a romantic table. That they were going to finally talk about what had been going on between them ever since they'd met. *You go, girl,* Elizabeth thought, giggling goofily while she brushed out the limp strands in the steady steam of heat so that they would stop looking like they were plastered to her forehead permanently. *Just don't go completely out of your gourd before you even make it downstairs.*

As she put back the blow-dryer in its drawer, her eye fell on an unopened package: It was the packet of birth-control pills she had shoved back into the corner after Finn had done his heart stomping.

Elizabeth stared at the pale orange plastic container. So innocent looking, yet such a big deal! That packet had the power to change her body. She recalled the research she'd done with Nina on birth-control pills. She'd learned quite a bit. She'd thought oral contraceptives were all she'd need if and when she was ready, until the health-clinic doctor had set her straight. Birth-control pills weren't even a hundred percent effective against the prevention of pregnancy—and they were zero percent effective against preventing sexually transmitted

diseases. Using condoms and birth-control pills together would be the safest bet, she'd been told.

It was all so complicated when it was brought
down to stuff like that. Stuff that wasn't romantic.
Stuff that had consequences. Serious consequences.

Elizabeth pulled the dispenser out of the
drawer and held it in her palm. She'd kept the pills
as a reminder of how close she'd come to doing
something stupid. Something she hadn't been
ready for emotionally, intellectually, or physically.
And even now, even though she was with a guy
she did trust, the pills still seemed scary.

Elizabeth opened the plastic cover and ran her
finger over the dial of pills. Would she ever use
these things? Or would she be a virgin for the rest
of her life? Okay, that sounded melodramatic even
to her. But when would she be ready?

School would be over in days. Summer was fast
approaching. Would she sleep with Sam one hot
summer night?

Suddenly a million tiny electric pulses ran up
and down her body.

Is that a sign? she wondered, smiling goofily
again into the mirror.

Elizabeth looked at her reflection, then down
at the pills again. Everything in her body whispered *yes* to the question of sex with Sam Burgess.

A whisper, not a scream. Which meant she was ready to think about it at least.

But a few months ago she'd thought—at least for a very little while—that she might be ready to sleep with Finn. She'd even told Finn she was ready, then changed her mind at the eleventh hour.

What if the same thing happened with Sam? What if he got upset the way Finn had? *No*, she told herself. *Two very different situations, two very different guys.* But would Sam be turned off by the fact that she had no idea what to do in the bedroom? She knew she wouldn't be able to fake it—even if she tried, she would only make a bigger fool of herself than if she admitted her complete ignorance. But Sam had been with lots of girls before, and he wasn't always—ahem—exactly Mr. Sensitive.

Elizabeth put the pills in the drawer, shoving them way in the back and placing some tissues over them. She could talk to Jessica, she supposed, but Jessica would just caution her about Sam's past and tell her Sam couldn't be trusted yet.

For the first time Elizabeth wished she had taken her sister's constant advice to read one of her *Cosmopolitan* magazines. There might be some advice there that would help Elizabeth think about the many components to a relationship. She could talk to Nina too.

Or she could trust her own instincts, which were telling her to trust Sam, to see this through, to give him a chance. If he messed up, if he lied to her, if he pulled anything remotely disrespectful, he was history.

After they talked tonight during dinner—really talked—she'd calm down and start being a citizen of her life again. No more wondering where Sam was or how he felt about her. Just an arm around her shoulders—and someone who was much more than a housemate and a friend.

Elizabeth sighed and gave her hair one final flip. Both her hair and her experience would have to do for now. This was it. Tomorrow she would go get some advice from Nina. Tonight she was going to let what happened happen.

Sam sat at the rickety table in his room, staring at the candles in a minor daze. What was the girl doing up there? he wondered. It had been quite a while since she'd surprised him and had run upstairs to "freshen up."

Feeling claustrophobic, he stood up, grabbed one of his trademark baseball caps, and headed out through the door that led into the kitchen. He just needed a little air, that was all. The sight of all the pots and pans crowding the sink only served to fortify whatever was motivating him to employ his escape hatch. Elizabeth slaving over a hot stove for him. The two of them staring across that stupid shining table and interlocking arms to drink from each other's wineglasses. He and Wakefield becoming a regular old boy-girl couple. Nix, nix, and nix.

Sam pushed through the swinging kitchen door and into the living room, then darted to the front door and burst outside, his heart pounding. The minute he breathed in the fresh air, he felt better. He stood on the porch in the gathering dark, barely able to make out the outline of the twins' Jeep in front of the house. Groups of SVU students heading out for a last Friday bash before finals made their way toward the quad, just a half mile away.

And here he was, where he always seemed to wind up—standing outside with his chest aching while he tried to figure out how to escape.

You know you're not going anywhere, Sam.

The voice was so strong, for a second Sam could have sworn that someone else really was speaking to him. He sat down on the steps, wishing that he could will away this weird sense of—of what? Panic? He felt sort of overwhelmed. That was it. Overwhelmed. Elizabeth was going to be down any minute. That was, if she wasn't in the process of turning herself into another Jessica makeup clone yet again.

161

You're afraid of intimacy. . . .

His friend Anna's words ran through his mind. He'd *yeah, right*ed Anna when she'd insisted his fear of a real relationship was the reason he was pushing Elizabeth away. But it was so true. Pathetically true. If he let Elizabeth in, in his heart and soul and all that stuff, she'd be in deep. She'd be too close. And if she met someone else, or discovered he was a jerk deep down, or just up and left him for whatever reason, he'd . . .

You'd what? he asked himself. *Be inconsolable, maybe.*

If he let himself need Elizabeth Wakefield, he could be in serious trouble.

Sam blew out a sigh and stared up at the night sky. What did it mean to *need* Elizabeth? He *didn't* need her. Sam didn't need someone depending on him for hugs and kisses, didn't need someone asking him where he was going every minute of the day, didn't need the hassle of a girlfriend in general. *Didn't. Need.* Period.

And Elizabeth doesn't need you either, he reminded himself. *She's gorgeous. She's brilliant. She's the most levelheaded person you know. She's got her own life, her own stuff going on. She doesn't need you for anything. She just likes you. That's all.*

Or maybe loves you.

Sam grinned sappily, surprising himself. So he

162

sort of liked the idea that someone he held in such regard could have those kind of feelings for him. But three seconds later he started feeling that claustrophobic way again, as though he were being backed into some imaginary corner.

So he could sit out here and allow his life to continue as it had before, with his most intimate relationships being Playstation and those two clue bags he called buds, Bugsy and Floyd. Or he could go inside and face his feelings—and have a totally amazing dinner besides.

He turned his baseball cap around and sighed. He didn't know if hearing someone burp and make all other kinds of disgusting noises could really pass for having "an intimate relationship." But it was true: Bugsy and Floyd were the closest thing he'd found to family ever since he'd quit contact with his own.

And as great as they are, they don't really complete *you, wouldn't you say, Sam?*

He cracked his knuckles, thinking of the scene in *Jerry Maguire* where a sweaty Tom Cruise told Renee Zellweger those fateful three words. When he had seen the movie, he'd totally identified with Jerry: He could see wanting to run as far away as possible from Renee and her kid. But he could imagine running through airports to get *Elizabeth* back. He could imagine wanting to talk to her, and only her, at the end of each day. He could even imagine saying the sappiest of sappy phrases to her one day: "You complete me."

So what was his problem?

Doofus, he told himself. *Your problem is that the last people who really expected anything of you—your family—wanted you to be someone you weren't. And you're worried Wakefield wants to run over you like a bulldozer too.*

Sam turned his baseball cap around again, leaning back to drink in the liquid night air. He was going to have to go inside in a second.

But Elizabeth didn't want him to be someone he totally wasn't. Did she?

Chapter Eleven

Chloe banged on Nina's door, too scared that she was going to see someone she knew to observe proprieties. Nina opened the door with her physics book still in her hand, looking like she was expecting to see a group of firemen and a blazing hallway outside. When she saw Chloe, she didn't look very relieved. "Chloe," she said, giving the shivering freshman the once-over. "What happened to you, girl?"

Chloe's teeth had begun to chatter. "Cold," was all she could force out, although how she'd managed to catch a chill in the balmy Sweet Valley evening was beyond her. "Can I come in?"

"Of course, of course," Nina said apologetically, stepping back and shaking her head while Chloe walked in and sat on the bed, hopping up and down slightly to keep warm. Nina closed the door behind her and turned to Chloe with a look of concern. Chloe cut her off before she could begin.

"Don't start," Chloe said, grabbing the coverlet, pulling it around herself, and trying to look Nina straight in the eye. "I know what you're going to say."

Nina crossed the room and sat down next to Chloe, putting a supportive hand on her knee. "I wasn't going to say anything," she said gently. "I was just going to try to find out what exactly happened here."

Nina's unexpected kindness brought on a totally fresh round of tears. Chloe had thought she had used them all up on the way home, but she clearly had more gulping and sobbing to do. Nina just watched and silently handed Chloe a tissue from her bedside table until she was ready to talk.

"It was *horrible*," Chloe finally forced out. "I can't believe I was so stupid."

Nina handed Chloe another tissue and watched while Chloe gave her nose an earth-shattering blow. "So stupid how?" she asked, very carefully.

Chloe looked at Nina, then down at her feet, which were still clad in the strappy sandals she'd picked out earlier in the evening to show off her legs. Ha! She kicked them off and tried to push them under the bed.

"So stupid," Chloe said, "as to believe that any guy would want to go out with me for *me*."

Nina looked like she was going to jump out with something very sharp but then rethought it and took another tack. She linked her arm with Chloe's. "Why don't you tell me exactly what happened," she said.

Chloe gave a shuddering sigh. "I don't *know*," she wailed, throwing up her hands in frustration. "After I saw you at the library, this totally hot guy asked me out for cappuccinos. It started out fine, but then he took me back to his apartment and was just *all over me*. And then it turned out that"— Chloe's voice rose suddenly to a fever pitch—"he only wanted sex. He wasn't interested in me at all. And it got worse, Nina. Really bad. He was all over me and he wouldn't stop and I had to run out—" Chloe broke down in a fresh round of sobs. "And I still don't have a date to the stupid semiformal!"

The expression on Nina's face was really scary. The girl looked like she'd kill the jerk if he happened by. "We should report him. Right now. Let's call." Nina jumped up and picked up the telephone.

"Nina," Chloe said, "call who? And it's not like anything happened. I mean, it's not like he ripped off my clothes or even touched skin. He just went too far, too fast, and I freaked."

Nina shook her head. "Chloe, if you hadn't run out when you did, he might have gone further." She put down the phone receiver. "I'm really sorry you had to go through that."

Chloe remained tensed for a second, then looked at Nina in disbelief. "That's it?" she said. "No lecture?"

Nina looked at Chloe quizzically. "Why would I want to give you a lecture? The only person I'd like to give a lecture to is that jerk, but he's not here, is he?"

Chloe reached over for another tissue and wiped off another handful of black soot. What was Nina up to? Was she just holding her deadly blow in abeyance?

"Well," Chloe said slowly. "How about, one, dressing up sexy is no way to meet guys; two, guys are not the be-all and end-all of the universe; and three, you're better off as dopey, boring, single Chloe."

Nina patted her on the back. "Well, I do agree with the second one," she said, forcing Chloe to rack her brains frantically to make sure that Nina hadn't just confirmed that she was dopey, boring, and doomed to terminal singleness. "But unfortunately, dressing up sexy is actually a *great* way to meet guys. It's the kind of guys you meet when that's *all* you do that can cause problems."

Chloe had no idea what Nina was talking about. "What do you mean?" she asked warily.

"Well," Nina said. "First of all, I don't know why you think that guys wouldn't want to date you." Chloe opened her mouth to retort that exactly the opposite was true, but Nina held up her hand to stop her. "You know, you don't give yourself enough credit, Chloe. You've grown up so much since you've been here. You've totally changed your rich-girl image; you got into Theta—which is, believe me, *not* easy—and you've made some great friends already, like Val and Jessica and—" Nina smiled. "And I guess, me. But you totally take the hard way every time."

Chloe sniffled into her tissue and wadded up the heap of them, padding over to the garbage can to throw away the heap. "What do you mean?" she asked.

Nina sighed and looked like she was choosing her words carefully. "Well, like the Theta thing," she said gently. "Everyone liked you, but you were nearly tripping over yourself trying to make sure you got in." Chloe blushed, hoping Nina wouldn't mention the Tom Watts thing from her first month at SVU. "Or the Tom Watts thing," Nina went on. "You didn't have to lie to get those girls to be impressed. They would have liked you fine if you'd just been yourself. But it's like you think you need

to be something better—or different—than you
are to get what you want."

Chloe closed her eyes, thinking of her mother's
constant pushing at her to get out there and sing
her own praises because nobody else was going to.
"But what does that have to do with tonight?" she
said, thinking of James's yucky tongue trying to
push itself practically down her throat.

"Well, instead of waiting around for a guy who
likes you or asking out a guy you like," Nina said,
"you change yourself into somebody you think a
guy will like. And when you do that, you pick up the
total bottom feeders. It's like dredging a lake instead
of using a fishing pole: You pull up *everything*."

Despite herself Chloe grinned at the image of
herself as a really bad fisherman. "So I've been
casting too wide a net?"

Nina started laughing. "Girl," she said. "Your
net could fit over half the heads in California."

The girls both burst out laughing. When
they'd finally subsided to just giggles, Chloe got
up the courage to ask the question that had really
been haunting her. "But how come," she said
haltingly, "if I'm so great, no one's asked me to
the semiformal yet?"

Nina's face got very serious. "Chloe, you can't
base your self-image on what guys do or don't do.
You're going to meet men that are really great and

men that you're going to want to vaporize by the time you get to really know them. And that's true of everyone. Dating isn't a matter of looking sexy or having blond hair or whatever. I mean, if that were true, Xavier would have married me and taken me away to live in a castle." Nina laughed, a short bark. "But I totally didn't get to know him, and he was just interested in me for my looks, it turned out." Nina sighed. "But that doesn't make me unlovable." She picked up one of her bed pillows and growled at it as if it were Xavier himself, slamming it into the bed. "It just makes him *one big jerk*."

Chloe wasn't sure she totally understood Nina one hundred percent, but she definitely felt better—especially since Nina had said that *she* was also her friend. "So, no more dressing sexy?" she said.

Nina smiled. "You can dress sexy or not," she said. "The clothes aren't to blame for that jerk's behavior—the jerk is to blame. But whatever you do, make sure you're doing it for yourself. Because if you don't know yourself, you can't really get to know anyone else."

Chloe thought deeply. What did that mean, know yourself? Did you just walk up to the mirror and introduce your face to its reflection? "But I don't have any idea how to get to know myself," she wailed.

Nina threw her arm around Chloe's shoulders.

"Well, after finals you might start studying up," Nina said conspiratorially. "Because at the end of the day you're your own best project."

"Here you go," Todd said to the bus driver, dropping a handful of coins into the bowl before he took a seat, still panting slightly.

Todd had caught the city bus just in time, running to catch the Plexiglas door before it slammed shut and guaranteed that he would *not* get to the dean's office in time to accomplish anything. Hopefully this would be the end of Todd's reign as king of the city buses. The end to a lot of things.

It was true that the drive to stop being a pampered rich boy—Beemer and bulging bank account and all—that had led him to work at Frankie's in the first place had been pretty good. He was nineteen, and that was too old to be sponging off his parents as if he were a five-year-old or something. He didn't want to be one of those trust-fund babies who hung out on the quad playing Hacky Sack all day, gunning off on the weekends in their eighty-thousand-dollar SUVs with thousands of dollars of sports equipment in the back, none of which they had paid for themselves. Todd's father and mother had both worked for everything they had, and he expected the same of himself: He was uncomfortable with things being handed to him on a platter.

But he'd totally gone over the edge. Acting like you had no more advantages than anyone else, Todd was beginning to realize, was *not* the way to become independent and self-made. He could work in Frankie's for the next fifty years, and that still wouldn't take away the fact that he had a rich mother and father. Working there until the end of time couldn't change that. Those were just the facts.

And it was incredibly stupid to throw *away* those advantages, Todd berated himself while the bus trundled through downtown Sweet Valley. What had all the people in Frankie's been saying to him since practically the day he'd walked in the door? That they would *kill* for some of the things he had: economic security, parents who paid for college, the opportunities his time at Sweet Valley afforded him. That's why they hadn't congratulated him when he'd joined the staff full-time. It didn't seem cool to them to just throw all that stuff away. It just seemed incredibly weird.

People without any advantages in life want to get somewhere despite that fact, Todd thought, almost laughing at how naive he had been and thinking of Rita, Cathy, and the rest of the hardworking gang over at Frankie's. *They don't want* company.

Especially not the company of scarily deluded rich

kids getting a degree in designer slumming.

The bus pulled up at the SVU gates, and Todd jumped out, almost flying over the asphalt as he sprinted toward student services. *Please be open,* he thought, clenching his teeth with exertion. *Don't make me wait for the weekend to get this thing done.*

He slammed open the building's French doors and ran toward the back office where he knew the dean of students reigned. The receptionist's chair was empty. *Dang,* Todd was thinking in disappointment when he saw the dean himself coming out of his office with his briefcase.

"Dean Strasser!" Todd exclaimed. "I've got to talk to you!"

The dean turned around, startled and not a little bemused. "I was about to pack it in," he said. "Todd, right?"

Todd gulped for air, standing in front of the door as if to physically prevent the dean from leaving. "Right, sir. Todd Wilkins. I'd like to be reinstated as a full-time student, starting the summer session. I need to make up courses."

The dean's normally dour face broke into a toothy smile. He straightened up and opened his door again, ushering Todd in. "Well, that *is* cause for celebration," he said broadly.

The dean walked behind his desk and put down his briefcase, taking some forms out of his drawer and handing them to Todd. "You'll need to fill all these out. If you hand them in by Monday, you'll still be able to enroll for summer and you can start back full-time in the fall. Now, may I ask," the dean said, smiling, "what precipitated this miraculous decision?"

Todd knew *precipitated* was an SAT word, but he'd totally forgotten what it meant. Still, he was pretty sure the dean was just asking what had changed his mind. He was more than ready to tell him.

"This is gonna sound really cheesy," Todd began, "but I realized I was burning bridges, not building them."

"An excellent metaphor, Wilkins." The dean laughed. "You've clearly only increased your brainpower with this little interruption. Sweet Valley University is only too happy to have you back."

Todd's head felt like it was going to burst—in a good way. Now was going to be the new era of Todd. He was going to keep his job at Frankie's—but part-time—and start looking around for a good used car that he could afford the payments on. He was going to work hard in his classes because working at Frankie's full-time was just as stupid and immature as expecting your parents to pick up the tab for the rest of your life, like those Hacky Sack jerks. And he was going to open his eyes and start appreciating what he'd been given instead of trying to throw it all away.

The dean stood and picked up his briefcase. "There isn't a person anywhere who won't congratulate you on this decision."

Todd thought about Rita, who was about to lose her assistant manager but gain a great part-time back-bar guy. Rita *would* be the first to congratulate him, he knew. That's how cool she was.

Todd stood up with his forms, pumping the dean's hand as if it were an oil derrick spouting black gold. "Thanks, sir."

The dean nodded. "I'm sure your parents will be thrilled with this news. They're going to be proud of you."

Todd smiled. He was proud too.

Jessica had sat on the couch so long, she was sure that the imprints of her spine and butt were going to be permanently ingrained on the soft cushions. *Well, worse things could stay there forever,* she thought, thinking of Sam's propensity for dribbling food and shoving half-finished sandwiches into all the furniture.

Jessica wondered what Elizabeth would do when she came downstairs to find her supposed boyfriend had blown out of here. Jessica had been sitting in this exact position when she'd spied Sam racing out of his room and outside. He hadn't come back.

He must really not be able to handle a relation-ship if he's ducking out on that dinner Liz is mak-ing, she thought. *Good riddance. I'll console my sister and get Sam's share of the meal.*

Why am I sitting here like a total loser? she asked herself. She hadn't felt like making plans for tonight after that scene with Elizabeth. But here she was, in her own house on a Friday night, wait-ing for her impossibly good-looking, incredibly gay friend to arrive and watch two lousy videos with her. What was wrong with this picture?

Well, first of all, Neil's not even here, Jessica thought sourly. She looked down at the cover of *My Best Friend's Wedding.* Julia Roberts absolutely glowed in a lavender dress that would have looked like a purple disaster on anyone else, with Rupert Everett smiling sardonically in the background like some evil, humorous genie.

"This is ridiculous," Jessica said aloud. She was one of the most popular, sought-after girls on campus, not some droopy wallflower. Why was she sitting around feeling sorry for herself?

I dunno, Jess. Maybe . . . duh . . . because you haven't gone out in—about a century?

"That's it!" Jessica crowed, glad to have found such a simple answer to her problem. Solutions, these days, were seeming scarcer than *Neil,* her supposed best friend. Well, she'd wanted tonight to be bonding central, but that clearly wasn't going to happen. She'd just have to go Jessica style and bump things up a notch.

An impromptu party would do it, she thought with glee. For a second the thought crossed her mind that her housemates might not feel like hosting a bunch of freeloaders in their living room. But she just as quickly dismissed it. Elizabeth and Sam were doing their own thing (if he ever came back, that was), and so—clearly—was Neil. Anyway, he wasn't here to speak for himself. Filled with sudden excitement and not a little bit of revenge mania for all her absent confidants, she picked up the phone and dialed Lila's number at Theta house.

"Hey, Li," she said after her friend's voice mail had kicked in. "Party at the house. Tell all the sisters, 'kay? And be there."

Well, Theta's taken care of, Jessica thought. Even if only her sorority came, it could still be a blast: like some slumber party run amok. Still, an infusion of menfolk couldn't hurt. After ruminating a second Jessica picked up the phone and called her frat contacts. *Party off campus, cool!* was everyone's response. She just had to leave a few more well-placed messages, sit back, and let the social tree of Sweet Valley do its wicked work. Jessica shoved a handful of Chee•tos into her mouth, smiling.

Suddenly the phone rang. *That was quick,* she thought, snatching up the receiver. "Party central!" she said.

"Hello?" a girl's voice replied. "Maybe I have the wrong number. I'm trying to reach Neil Martin?"

"Oops, sorry," Jessica told her. "Right number, but Neil's not home. Can I take a message for him?"

Jessica wondered if she should mention the party to this friend of Neil's, whoever she was. Jessica decided discretion would be best—Neil might hate the girl, whoever it was. She was beginning to get geared up for a total blowout.

"Yeah, can you tell him Mona called and that I'm really sorry, but my roommate changed her mind and isn't moving out after all. So the room's not available anymore. Tell him I'll rip up the check he gave me for first and last month's rent."

Huh? The first month's rent. Jessica was rendered wordless—literally. "Okay," she finally gasped, replacing the phone in its cradle.

Jessica stared unseeingly into space. "I'll do that," she whispered to the empty room.

Neil was moving out? Since when?

Jessica realized that some kind of blowout *besides* her party must have already happened at the house, right under her very nose.

* * *

Nina's head drooped over her physics book. She shook herself to get back a little energy. *Of which is the determining principle . . . ,* she read, for what had to be the fortieth time. With a gusty sigh she slammed the book closed. Studying was over. For tonight at least.

Tapping her pencil on the book's shiny cover, Nina thought about the conversation she'd just had with Chloe. Comforting weeping Chloe, her eyes raccooned by all the makeup she'd had on, had been like giving herself a little wake-up lecture too. Not that she'd told Chloe that. Not that she'd even realized it herself at the moment.

Looking down at her ratty old sweatshirt and frayed jeans, Nina had to laugh. *If I'm my own project, I get a C-minus,* she thought. But mixing school and social hour had only spelled disaster for her, right?

Well, you are *a physics major, Ms. Harper,* Nina chided herself. *If you don't know how to make point a connect to point* b, *you've* really *been wasting your big, fat scholarship.*

The phone rang, and Nina grabbed it. "Hello?"

"Hi, Nina? It's me, Chloe."

"Hey, Chlo. You okay?"

"Yeah. Thanks to you. Hey, I thought you'd want to know that there's a party at the Wakefields'. I'm gonna go. Are you?"

Nina frowned. Elizabeth hadn't called her to invite her. *That* was weird. The girl was her best friend! Maybe Elizabeth didn't know there was a party. It was totally Jessica-like to call a party and not tell the other housemates. "Chloe, I'm not sure if I can make it, but maybe I'll see you there."

"Okay, bye!" Chloe chirped, and hung up.

Nina replaced the receiver in the cradle. She'd done a good job with Chloe, she realized. Otherwise the freshman wouldn't be up for the party. The girl was resilient. *The way we all have to be,* Nina reminded herself.

Feeling reinvigorated, Nina shucked off her old study duds and grabbed her shower caddy. A hot shower of suds was just what she needed to wake herself up—in every way. She was supposed to have learned a lesson about partying when she should be studying. *But it's Friday night,* she reminded herself. *And you don't have to stay out till all hours. You can go out, have some fun, be social, and be in the library at nine* A.M.

As she lathered up her hair, Nina began to formulate a new theory of her social life. *I just went too far in one direction, like Chloe,* she thought, wincing at the thought of how pale and rattled Chloe had been when she'd come to her door. It was enough to turn a girl off dating forever, but Nina had worked through too many difficult physics equations to just

181

turn her back on things when they seemed insolvable. The trick, she realized, rubbing a pumice stone over her toes and heels, was the same one she had used countless times in her incredibly difficult classes: You just had to keep working through problems until your brain got the hang of things and finally found the solution.

But what's my solution? Nina thought as she padded down the hallway back to her room. Throwing her robe on her bed, she told herself not to worry about it right now. She took her favorite lavender-scented lotion and began rubbing it over her newly shaven legs. *Stick with the basics, and the rest will come.*

Throwing open her closet, Nina looked to see what kind of concept she could work for the evening. The black minidress was way too extreme—anyway, it reminded her of the outfit she had worn the night she'd met Xavier. Ditto for the spangly V-necked top and matching boot-leg pants. Her knee-length suede skirt, though, Nina realized, pulling it out of the logjam of clothes, might be perfect. Paired with a teeny cotton top with puffed sleeves and her dark boots, the whole thing might be pretty fabulous.

Zipping up both boots, Nina checked her reflection in the mirror. Excellent! Subdued, yet very sexy at the same time. Now for the hair. She squeezed a generous dollop of ProV—the conditioner in a bottle that made it look like plasma—into her palm. Working it through until all her long curls felt springy yet controlled, Nina pulled out a few curls to frame her face and decided to let her hair air dry for maximum volume.

Nina debated whether the outfit really called for makeup. Without it she might look a little too reserved, she decided. *Anyway, moderation in all things,* she reminded herself.

Using a lip liner to secure the lipstick, Nina applied some raspberry-tinted color to her lips with a brush, tilting her head to make sure she'd filled in the lines correctly. A little mascara, a light dusting of powder, and she was done—the makeup was a far cry from the sort of siren shades that she'd layered over the planes of her face earlier this year, but it was also a far cry from plain-faced, mousy Nina in her decided unchic glasses—the only Nina most of the world had ever seen.

Giving her curls a final shake, Nina looked at herself in the full-length mirror hanging on the closet door, completely satisfied. *Okay, definite B-plus, maybe even an A-minus,* she thought merrily. *Now, my learned one, you just have to make good use of your newfound knowledge.*

Chapter
Twelve

Sam pulled open the door, shut it, then squared his shoulders and took a deep breath. *Jeez, Burgess, you're not facing the firing squad. It's a girl! Just one incredible girl who you've been running from for almost a year now.*

He took a deep breath, inhaling the amazing aroma of baked salmon and other delicious-smelling food, then pushed through the kitchen's swinging door. Elizabeth was standing in the kitchen, arranging the fish on a plate with what looked like sprigs of parsley (Sam had never been too knowledgeable about the herb kingdom).

She looked stunning. She wore some kind of skimpy white dress, and her hair was streaming down her back, just the way he liked it. She wasn't wearing any makeup, but her face was flushed from all of her exertions. She looked like some kind of adorable country girl out of a novel or a totally hot movie star on vacation at a Caribbean resort.

Lingering over the vision of her lean, tanned arms and shapely calves before she noticed him standing there like some drooling fool, Sam couldn't believe how beautiful she was. Even better, he knew that the person inside that body was just as wonderful. How had he been about to run away from *that*?

He must have made some kind of noise because Elizabeth looked up and gave a little jump. "Oh!" she said. "I was so absorbed in this that I didn't even hear you come in. I was wondering where you were." She took a bite of a sprig of parsley. "Are you hungry?"

"Starved," Sam said, his throat dry.

"Great. Everything's ready. Why don't you bring in the ice bucket?"

Grabbing the filled bucket off the counter, Sam followed Elizabeth through the door leading into his room. Despite the major therapy session he'd had with himself outside, he still couldn't help but feel—slightly—that he was being led to the electric chair, not to the miniparadise she'd labored so hard to create. How did he let her know that while he appreciated the effort, this was totally not his style?

"There," she said, placing the salmon in the center of the table. Bowls and plates of other steaming delicacies had crowded the small surface so that it couldn't hold another thing. Grabbing the bottle of wine by its neck, Sam plucked it off the tabletop and put it in the bucket. Debating a moment, he placed it on his desk, within arm's reach. He had almost sat down when his formal upbringing reared its ugly head.

"For the chef." He pulled out Elizabeth's chair with a flourish. *Argh*. Where had *that* come from?

"*Merci*, monsieur," she said, her eyes shining. Sam ripped his cap off his head, tossed it onto his bed, then sat down, feeling like he should be wearing a tie and tails. "This seems to bring out the best in you," she joked. "Maybe I should do it more often."

That's exactly what you should not *do,* Sam thought. The renewed panic he'd felt the moment they'd entered his room was getting worse. *Be cool, man, be cool,* he told himself, feeling like the undercover cop in *Pulp Fiction*.

Sam cleared his throat. "This was great of you to do this, Elizabeth. But—"

"Don't talk," Elizabeth cut in, giving him a smile that rendered him unable to continue. She gestured at the wine bucket. "Pour."

Sam nodded like an automaton, fumbling with

the now slippery bottle and the corkscrew she handed him. He finally popped the cork and poured them each a brimming glass. He, for one, knew he would need it. "Again, um, this is great. But it's totally—"

Elizabeth tilted her head, her eyes narrowed. "It's totally what?" She placed a filet on each of their plates and began to spoon rice onto his. "Too much? Too much for *you*?"

Mind reader. Well, wasn't that one of the reasons he and Elizabeth had this amazing chemistry in the first place? She could read him; they both knew that. Not many people could. And she challenged him—always. Sometimes she knew when to let him off the hook, drop whatever issue was bugging her. Elizabeth Wakefield wasn't just another girl he could control or manipulate to suit his needs.

But no matter what, he wanted to get this thought out, whatever happened. He couldn't let her go on thinking he was Mr. Moonlight and Roses when he was more like Mr. Pepperoni and Extra Cheese.

"Well, it's not really me, Wakefield," he said. "All this fine dining and gooey stuff just makes me kind of . . . uncomfortable. I'm sort of surprised you didn't know that."

A look of extreme unhappiness crossed her face

for a second, but she hid it quickly with a faltering smile. "Of course I knew. But hey, you haven't even tried the rice yet. I'm sure it's not *that* gooey."

Sam smiled despite himself. The girl knew how to handle him. That was for sure. Here she was, being great while he fumbled every pass like a big jerk. He took a deep breath and a sip of wine. "But Elizabeth, I don't want all this stuff," he burst out. "Candles. Romance. Whatever. It makes me feel like—"

"Like you're doing something you're not into for the sake of someone else?" she thrust in, popping a bite of salmon into her mouth. "Like you're expected to appreciate it? Like you're obligated to give something back?"

Elizabeth's constant interruptions caught Sam off guard, but he preferred this sort of biting dialogue to the grim evening of sweet nothings and violins he had been fearing. At least this was *real*.

Ah, his favorite words: *expectations* and *obligations*. "Maybe," he said, at last shoveling a spoonful of rice into his mouth. Whatever else he might say about her, Elizabeth could definitely wield a spatula. "But what I really mean is, um . . . we don't need all this stuff. Fancy little dinners with tablecloths. Big-deal breakfasts out at Yum-Yums.

You wearing more makeup than Jessica." Oops. That last bit had just kind of slipped out. He hoped he wasn't about to get a handful of asparagus tips across his head just for being honest.

Instead of looking angry, Elizabeth looked kind of amused. "You don't think I clean up well, Burgess?"

"You know you're a goddess," Sam said. That had also come out before he could stop it. He had certainly thought that hundreds of times, but he hadn't had any intention of ever telling her so. "You don't need any makeup. And we don't need any of this." He swept his arm around the table.

Elizabeth smiled, then looked down, then back up at him. Was she going to let him have it? "Look, Sam, I know this isn't your style. But it's *mine*. I dealt with your style plenty this past year. So, can you do me this one favor and eat some great food on a nicely set table and like it?"

Sam had to hand that one to her. She had him there. He grinned. Man, she could be totally cool. "You've got a deal." He reached out a hand and covered hers with his own. An electric shock passed through Sam. They sat there for a moment, and then she pulled her hand away.

Elizabeth pushed a silken strand of blond hair behind her ear. "I only made us this dinner so that we'd be forced to talk. In private." She looked

Sam full in the eye and took a sip of her own wine. A *big* sip.

Ah, there it was! Sam knew there had been something he'd wanted to object to—or complain about. It was all this stupid talk-talk-talking that he knew he'd have to do if he went out with Elizabeth. "Why do you want to talk so much, Wakefield? Why do you have to know every little thing?"

She raised an eyebrow.

Oh. Yeah. That's right. Suddenly he felt like an idiot. He'd promised her he'd tell her about his family, about his reasons for keeping their wealth a secret, about why he'd taken off after their kiss those months ago. She was calling him on it, and he was acting like she was asking too much. *Are you this freaked about having a real relationship?* he asked himself. *Yeah, guess so.*

Before he could say anything else, Elizabeth leaned toward him. "I'll tell you why. Because I *like* you, Sam. I like you big time. And because you owe me some hard truths, no matter how tough it is for you to spill your personal life story. I want to *know you better* before this relationship of ours goes any further. Ever hear of that?" She leaned back, waiting.

As ready as he had been to jump down her throat, Sam couldn't help but feel totally blown

190

away by Elizabeth's response. She wasn't trying to make him over. She was trying—with some salmon and a bottle of wine—to get this relationship started. The relationship they'd both wanted but had been too afraid of for a year. He thought of all the times he had scornfully looked at couples deeply engaged in conversation, thinking that the women must be tearing answers out of the men with the verbal equivalent of fishhooks. But it had never occurred to him that couples could really *talk* in some kind of mutually beneficial way—not just fight, make cooing noises, or be ironically distant.

Sometimes, Burgess, he thought, *you even shock yourself with how dense you are about the world of love and Elizabeth Wakefield.*

She met his silence calmly, picking up an asparagus spear with her fingers. "Did I make a mistake with you again, Sam?"

"Meaning?" he asked, pushing his rice around with his fork.

Elizabeth glanced down at her plate, then back up at him. "Well, it seems to me that you don't want to be here, that you can't deal with an ice bucket or a real conversation."

"But—"

"Yeah, *but.* That's all you've been saying tonight. *Yeah, but.* You've been trying your hardest to make me angry or push me away or make

191

me get up and tell you it's over before it's started. Am I right? Because if that's the case, Sam, if that's what you really want, I have a twin sister who'd be really into your portion of this meal and who'd be really happy to hang out with me tonight and watch a movie. So what's it gonna be, Burgess? Are we going to talk and have a relationship, or are we going to be housemates and forget about this whole thing?"

Sam stared at her. She held his gaze with those amazing blue-green eyes, the ones that he could never fool, the ones that knew him, the ones that were asking him to take this chance. *What you do now marks your path with this girl*, he told himself. *You walk out, that's it. You stay, and you've got yourself a girlfriend who you'd better learn to deal with*.

She bit off the green head of another piece of asparagus. She wasn't staring at him with tears in her eyes. She wasn't waiting on pins and needles for his big answer. *She doesn't need you*, he reminded himself. *She just likes you. Maybe even loves you*.

"So, um, I owe you a long, boring story about me and my family," he said finally.

She froze midbite and looked at him, her expression full of relief and joy.

"Okay," he said simply, surprising himself yet again. "Here's what happened."

* * *

As Sam took a life-story-postponing sip of wine, Elizabeth felt like she should be wearing a skimpy leotard and top hat and carrying a big whip. *But lion tamers have it easy compared to this,* she thought, looking across the table at her very own personal lion. Sam was getting ready to tell her the big saga of his life. And it had taken every ounce of her conversational acumen to get it out of him.

Fortunately, sparring with Sam this way was kind of . . . fun.

She had to admit she had also had her doubts about the two of them being able to jump into some lovey-dovey kind of rapport straight from the *Jerry Springer*-esque screaming matches they'd been engaging in lately. But it seemed like she didn't have to put in any extra pushing and pulling to fit their conversation into a romantic mold. It had a very organic—and very weird— shape of its own: kind of like a rose with all the thorns still sticking out of it.

Well, that's okay, Elizabeth thought. She knew she could be intense, and Sam was definitely a complex little nut to crack. She hadn't expected their dinner to have the kind of swoonlike silkiness of her nights with Finn. And she didn't want it to, she knew. She wanted the real thing, and she was getting it. Thorns and all.

Sam cleared his throat a couple of times. She knew not to interrupt while a person was getting ready to begin—one false move, and you had to start all over again. So she simply waited. And waited.

"So," Sam began. "I have this older brother, Morgan. I used to worship him. He was a really great guy. But my father put a lot of pressure on him." Sam paused.

Elizabeth decided it was safe to jump in. "What kind of pressure?"

It was like a dam had cracked—suddenly all the words came out in one massive rush. "My dad's this cold corporate tycoon—we're talking *no* human qualities to speak of, and he wanted Morgan to be the same way. And to go into the family businesses, of course. But Morgan wasn't like my father. He was quiet, into drawing, art, music."

Sam paused again, seeming lost in thought for a moment. Elizabeth imagined he was thinking about Morgan, about the brother he'd looked up to.

Sam cleared his throat, then continued. "He probably would've joined the Peace Corps or something. He was always talking about helping the underdog. But my dad intimidated the guy like you wouldn't believe and turned my gentle brother into some miniversion of our dad.

Morgan's now exactly like my father, but maybe even more ruthless. He treats his own little kids the way my parents treated us: like we're meant to be seen and not heard."

Elizabeth stared at him, not wanting to say anything that might make him stop talking.

He took a deep breath. "So, with Morgan all whipped into Burgess shape, my parents turned their psycho sights on me. My father had everything set up for me: the colleges I would be allowed to consider attending, the acceptable majors, internships at one of his corporations, the career path, everything. I could barely go to the bathroom if it wasn't on his schedule," Sam said, smiling a little.

Elizabeth swallowed. "Then what happened?"

"Well, then I turned eighteen," he explained. "And became a legal adult, able to make my own decisions. I told my folks I had no intention of following in their footsteps. That I'd make it on my own, my own way. My father and brother laughed in my face, told me I was an immature kid who'd amount to nothing. That I'd be back, begging for the good life. I've proved them wrong for two years."

"And you've had no contact with them in all this time?" Elizabeth asked.

Sam nodded. "Last year I got one letter from

my mother telling me I was a disappointment and that I'd better stop 'this nonsense right now.' I wrote back that I didn't consider living my life my way to be 'nonsense.' My dad called soon after and left some obnoxious message on my machine, saying I had no right to talk to my mother like that, who did I think I was, blah, blah, blah. Whatever. I kept expecting my brother to stand up for me, to be proud of me for doing what he'd wanted to but couldn't. But I never heard from him."

Elizabeth was so stunned that she couldn't speak. It wasn't because she had no words for how lonely that situation sounded; it was because all the questions in her mind were trying to surface at the exact same time.

"So how *do* you live?" she asked. "How have you paid for anything?"

Sam looked at her, cocking an eyebrow. "Don't worry, Wakefield," he said. "I'm not running guns or anything. My grandfather left me a little bit of money as a trust for college, so I feel okay using that. It's small beans, but it pays my way."

Her mind still whirling, Elizabeth merely nodded. No wonder Sam never talked about his past. This wasn't the kind of story you whipped out over a turkey sub and a six-pack.

He looked at her, his expression serious, almost

anguished. "I'm sorry about everything that happened two months ago. I'm sorry I freaked about that kiss. I'm sorry I took off. I'm sorry you caught me in what looked like a compromising situation—that I let you think for a second anything was going on with me and another girl." Sam looked down, then back up at her. "There has never been another girl since I met you last summer."

Elizabeth gasped.

"I mean, I've been with other girls, yes. But never, not once, has a girl gotten inside me. Not once have I ever wanted to have a relationship with anyone else. You've—"

Elizabeth waited on pins and needles, but she didn't think Sam would finish his sentence. "I've what?"

"You've . . . changed me," he finally said. "I guess for the better, but it feels weird."

Elizabeth laughed. "Yeah, I think you've been making that perfectly clear."

Sam smiled, then his expression turned serious again. "But I'm not gonna let anyone tell me what to do. So if you don't like this guy here, Wakefield, tell me now. Because I'm going to live my life according to *my* rules—not my parents' and not yours."

Elizabeth knew not to take the vehemence in his voice personally. That was one of the things that *Sam* had taught *her*. To look behind the tone or the words for what was really going on in the person's head. "I don't want you to live by my rules, Sam. A relationship is about mutual respect, about wanting to make the other person happy while not compromising yourself or your values. Don't you agree?"

"Yeah," he said. "Yeah. That's exactly how I'd define a good relationship."

Elizabeth let out the breath she was holding. "So you don't have to worry so much about me trying to change you. I just don't want to feel like every time I take a step toward you, you take four steps back."

Sam nodded. "I'll work on it. I promise you that."

She looked down at their half-finished meal, then across the table at Sam. "Want to work on it upstairs?" she asked. "I've got a big, comfy bed that's perfect for talking away the night on."

He stared at her. "You *sure* you want to deal with the likes of me? A penniless slacker who goes to community college and doesn't know what he wants to be? A guy who's sure to drive you crazy, even if he doesn't mean to?"

Elizabeth felt her heart constrict in her chest. She smiled at him, afraid she'd cry. "Yeah, I'm sure."

She stood up, and so did he.

Sam glanced down at the table. "I'll wash the dishes since you cooked."

Elizabeth shook her head. "They can wait till later."

"I was hoping you'd say that," Sam said, holding out his arm. "Ready . . . sweetheart?"

Elizabeth could feel the pinpricks of tears of joy at the backs of her eyes. All she could do was nod.

Chloe sat in the center of her bed, feeling like a new woman after her talk with Nina. Instead of sinking into the self-pity fest she'd envisioned herself indulging in on her walk home from James's place, she felt weirdly elated, like someone *had* asked her to the semiformal. Well, someone had, sort of. She was considering asking herself. *Wow,* she thought. *I sound like a self-help book!*

And she *was* going to Jessica's party tonight. She'd spent this entire school year trying to earn the right to be invited to a party at Jessica Wakefield's house. And when she'd gotten back to her sorority house tonight, there'd been a message from Jessica *herself.* Chloe hadn't heard about the party secondhand. She'd been invited by the big cheese herself! The pledge chairwoman of Theta, one of the most popular girls at SVU, a sophomore to boot, obviously considered Chloe a real friend if she left a message for her personally.

And that was all Chloe had wanted from SVU: friendship.

Chloe grabbed a shopping bag from earlier and swept all of her new cosmetics into it. She shimmied out of her outfit and put all her new clothes—including the bra she had been wearing—into the rest of the bags. Then she donned her robe and fluffy slippers and marched into the common room, which was filled with dozens of quietly studying Thetas, all with their heads bent over books.

"Free stuff!" she announced, dumping everything on the center of the floral-patterned rug.

The room erupted. Chloe walked to the door, watching the Thetas rip through her new purchases like kids at a piñata party. *Well, that's that,* Chloe thought, giggling.

Loving the pins and needles of what felt like her hundredth shower that day, Chloe scrubbed her face hard enough to remove a couple of layers of skin to get off all traces of icky, grody James. Back in her room, she donned her favorite worn jeans and her comfiest vintage cardigan and slipped her feet into her beat-up mules. Then she pulled her hair back in a tight, wet ponytail. Wasn't there a cosmetic line or something called Back to Basics? Well, that was her for now.

She looked in the mirror. *This* was Chloe Murphy. This was the girl she'd wanted to be when she'd arrived at SVU back in September. And this was the girl she was proud to be. Take *that,* world.

She left her room and headed out, planning to walk the half mile to Jessica's house. She felt so confident, so full of positive energy that she almost skipped her way through the quad.

"Hey, Chloe!"

She turned at the sound of her name. Chloe was slightly deflated to see Val and Martin—holding hands, of course—emerging from the grim depths of the library. The new Chloe would appreciate a guy like Martin. Appreciate his crush on her. Appreciate the fun they'd had. But the old Chloe had let him go. And a better girl had won his heart.

"Chloe!" Val screamed, running over and throwing her arms around Chloe's neck. "I feel like I haven't see you in forever!" Martin joined them, his eyes shining.

Chloe felt her heart inflate at Val's greeting. "Hey! Hi, Martin," Chloe said. "Long time, no see, bud."

Martin held out his arms, and Chloe flew into them for a bear hug. They stood there, grinning at each other like idiots.

"So where are you guys going?" Chloe asked.

"They're showing *Breakfast at Tiffany's* at the student center," Val said, smiling broadly. "I've seen it five thousand times, but I have to see it every time it's on the big screen." She was practically jumping up and down with excitement. "Wanna come?"

"I would love to," Chloe said, "but Jessica actually called me herself to invite me to her party, and hey, Val, you know what that means to me!"

Val grinned, and Chloe was struck by what an incredible friendship the two of them had built. They'd been through so much together. And Chloe hadn't been afraid to tell Val the truth about the party—that she was proud to be invited. The old Chloe would have tried to make herself sound impressive.

"Okay, go have fun," Val said. "Maybe we'll see you later at Starlights or Yum-Yums."

Martin kissed Chloe good-bye on the cheek, then slipped his arm around Val's shoulders and led her off in the direction of the student center.

Chloe watched them go. She loved both those people, she realized. *Loved* them. They were her friends. Real friends. She wouldn't take that for granted ever again. Jessica, Val, Martin, Nina. Those were her buds now. And maybe Chloe would even make some new friends now that she'd finally gotten the clue she'd always thought she had.

So I've learned something my freshman year after all, she thought, grinning stupidly to herself.

The sound of an approaching group of chatting girls and a few guys caught Chloe's attention, and she turned around. She recognized a few Thetas, and one of them, Sue, smiled at her.

"Headed to Jessica's?" Sue asked Chloe.

"Yeah," Chloe said. "You guys too?"

Sue nodded and took a pack of gum out of her little purse. "Want some?" she asked, offering the pack to Chloe.

"Sure," Chloe told her. "Never know who you'll kiss later!"

The girl laughed, and Chloe fell into step beside her. And for the first time since September, Chloe Murphy felt like an individual *and* part of a group.

Chapter
Thirteen

Jessica lay back on the couch, feeling like she'd been mummified for the past thousand years and only recently let out for air.

She still couldn't believe she'd heard correctly. Neil was moving out? Her best buddy? How could that *be*? They'd had their share of trials, Jessica knew, but ever since they'd met, Jessica and Neil had gone together like peanut butter and fluff. White on rice. Rupert and Julia, for crying out loud.

Jessica rubbed at an imaginary pinpoint on her forehead, wishing she could bore a hole into her brain and rip out the last thirty minutes, erasing them forever from history. In fact, she'd make it the last year. So she'd never have met Neil and never had to live through him moving out on her.

Slow down, Jess, she told herself. *You don't know for sure what's happening.*

Oh, yeah? the other side of her brain responded. *Well, assuming Neil wasn't renting a room so he'd have a pied-à-terre in downtown Sweet Valley, it looks like you've lost a housemate and best friend. Or you* were *going to lose one,* she corrected herself, remembering that that girl—what was her name, Mona?—had said the room wasn't available anymore. Neil clearly wanted to move out. If this Mona person's room wasn't available anymore, he'd surely find another one.

Jessica let out a sigh big enough to blow away small objects, wondering if it would be possible to duck out of her own party. People would probably be arriving in an hour or so—what if she *just wasn't there? Nice try,* she thought. *Strangers might not notice, but all of your friends are going to think it's strange if they can't find the hostess at her own party.* She smirked, picturing herself hiding under the kitchen cabinets while Sam and Elizabeth were interrupted by a rowdy crowd knocking ceaselessly. *No, we certainly can't depend on the lovebirds to hold up their end of the social contract, now, can we?*

What was going on around here? Just a few weeks ago Jessica and Neil had been as thick as ever, and Sam and Elizabeth hadn't been able to even stay in the same room with each other for five seconds. Now Elizabeth and Sam were engaged in some gustatory pleasure fest that had evidently moved from Sam's room up to Elizabeth's bedroom, Jessica was alone on the couch, and Neil was, evidently, calling girls with names like Mona to get away from girls named Jessica.

Jessica couldn't even take solace in the fact that Neil was moving out to be alone. Wherever he was going, he clearly didn't have a problem with housemates in general—only with the ones he had now. "Unreal," Jessica muttered, wondering when everything had gotten so screwed up.

She heard the front door open, then close. Unless this was some really eager party goer who knew how to jimmy locks, there was only one person that could be.

Neil's footsteps sounded through the kitchen like gun reports. He stopped, clearly perplexed by the rare silence, then continued down the hallway into the living room. Jessica wasn't facing the doorway, but she could tell he was standing in it. He was quiet for a moment, then she could hear him walk around and sit in front of her.

"Jessica," Neil said.

She realized that tears were streaming down her face. This was ridiculous—she'd *just* had a big bawl fest with her sister.

"Jessica," Neil said again. "I—"

"You had a message," she cut him off. "Someone named Mona."

"I know," Neil said. "I called her to check in before I came home. Jess, I—"

She turned to face him, trying to stop another round of tears from brimming over her eyes and down her face. "Neil, what's going on?" she said. "What's happening?"

Neil sighed deeply, his hands in his pockets. The only good thing Jessica could think of about the situation was that she knew Neil would answer her. In her opinion, one of the many advantages to being close with a gay man versus a straight one was that he wouldn't run away from an argument. In fact, it was she who usually ran away. But this time she was too upset to do any running.

Neil waited awhile before he spoke. When he did, it was clear and concise. "I was having a lot of problems living with all of you," he said finally. "There was just too much fighting. I couldn't take it anymore."

Jessica just looked at him, feeling like that was such a lame explanation for sneaking around your best friend's back and trying to totally *escape*. "That's all?" she wailed. "Why didn't you say anything?"

"I *did*," Neil said, his incredibly gray eyes and chiseled face somber. "You just weren't listening."

Jessica thought back to all the times she'd talked to Neil in the past few months. Well, maybe she had been unloading on him a little. But that's what friends were for, wasn't it?

"Neil, I don't understand," she said. "You were going to throw away our whole friendship because things were a little intense? Isn't our friendship worth more than that to you?"

The question brought on a round of fresh weeping. Neil's face darkened, as if in pain. "Jessica, I wasn't going to throw away our friendship," he said slowly. "I just wanted a little—peace and quiet."

Jessica couldn't contain herself. That was the most ridiculous thing she'd ever heard. "You were just going to unexpectedly move out—because of me—and you didn't think that was going to put a crimp in our relationship?" she exploded.

Neil ducked his head, then looked up again, his eyes burning. "I knew it was going to be hard," he said. "But I thought we'd get through it. Anyway, it wasn't just you," he added after a minute.

Jessica's head flew up. "Oh, so you also have a problem with my sister?" she hissed.

Neil laughed. "Now you're suddenly Elizabeth's defense team? Since when?"

"Since she started going out with that jerk we call a housemate, and—"

Neil raised an eyebrow. "Well, now you see

what I mean. I had to live through almost a year of their fighting and sniping, constantly being asked to jump in the middle. Now I have to deal with you being upset they hooked up. How am I supposed to study? How am I supposed to get any sleep? I'm not into taking yoga to destress. I want peace in my own house."

"But—"

Neil held up a hand. "It wasn't any one person who made me want to flee this nuthouse. It was the dynamic. Which was *heinous*."

Okay, okay, Jessica couldn't disagree with that one. She had been screaming at Neil about it for weeks, hadn't she?

"Well, when were you planning to tell me?" Jessica asked. "After the moving truck arrived?"

"Jessica, that's what I'm trying to tell you," Neil said. "I wasn't going to tell you at all. Because I had already decided not to go through with it."

Jessica narrowed her eyes at her best friend. "Okay, this had better be good. Or you've got some serious groveling to do now that your escape hatch isn't available."

Neil almost laughed at the sight of Jessica, hands on hips, awaiting his big explanation. The girl had such a happy, open face that an angry expression on her was almost comical.

But he'd been telling the truth. He *had*

changed his mind. Neil had picked up the phone to call Mona to tell her he wasn't taking the room after all, could he please have his check back, when she'd told him she'd just left him a message saying the room wasn't available.

Talk about fate.

It was like so many things in his life, he was beginning to realize. After he'd outed himself as gay to the entire student body during his campaign for student-body president last semester, he realized that he hadn't been afraid to tell everyone that he was gay. In fact, he had been *searching* for some way to tell people. He was sick of having such an essential part of himself be some sort of major secret. All of his angsting around had just been impatience at getting it out in the open—not fear.

It was a similar situation to his moving out. The minute the deed was truly done—and the minute Neil had known confronting Jessica about the problems he was having was inevitable—he'd realized he didn't really want to move out at all. He had just needed a way to tell her what he was feeling.

And so Neil had called Mona immediately. When she'd picked up the phone, she started apologizing over and over. After a minute he'd realized that he wasn't going to have to duck out on her after all. Fate had done his work for him.

But when Mona had told him that she'd left a

message with one of his housemates, Neil had figured it was probably Jessica who had gotten the call. That would have been fate too. And it had been.

He'd known that he'd have to talk to her about the problems he was having in the house. That was all he'd wanted to do in the first place—which he would have realized if he hadn't been such a high-strung doofus. A few minutes ago he'd told Jessica that he'd been trying to tell her all along that he couldn't take the constant emotional roller coaster living here required. But he hadn't. Anytime he got frustrated, he simply headed out to the library or to a friend's dorm or to Yum-Yums. By deciding to move out instead of trying to fix a problem, he'd gone for the easy route instead of the right route. Again.

And he'd hurt his best friend. He knew she'd be able to forgive him, but he hoped it didn't take too long. Because if there was anything he didn't want, it was more tension in the house.

Neil realized that he'd just thought through everything he needed to tell Jessica. That was his problem. He thought instead of said. He took a deep breath, led Jessica over to the hideous daisy-print sofa, plopped her down, and told her everything on his mind.

"Jessica," he concluded, looking at his favorite girl at SVU, her eyes red rimmed and her hair half coming out of her ponytail. "You're my best friend. I love you. You're stuck with me whether you like it or not."

Jessica let out a shuddering breath. "Good. 'Cause I want to be stuck with you."

"And next time," Neil said, "I won't be reluctant to get in another big fight. I'll just yell at you and let you yell back, and then we'll go for burritos or mocchacinos."

Jessica laughed. "So what are you going to do the next time you just can't bear to talk to me?" she said. "Get a girlfriend?"

"A really gorgeous one," Neil said. "With big bazooms and everything. Then you'll *know* we have to talk."

Jessica grinned. "Well, I'll try to step in before the marriage. Hey, so what's in the Max Out bag?" She gestured at the plastic bag with the electronic store's logo.

"I got you a present." Neil pulled two beepers from the bag. "I got them when I thought I wanted to move out. But I think they'll still come in handy. This one's for you." He handed her the red one. "And this is for me. So you can find me anywhere— like if I'm in an ashram recovering from your sister and Sam having a lover's spat, for instance."

Jessica gave him a look. "Oh, I'll be there with you, buddy boy," she said. "Don't you worry."

They both burst into laughter, then gave each other a long, deep hug. "Neil?" Jessica said.

"Mm-hm?" Neil managed to croak out, considering his face was crushed into Jessica's ponytail.

"Will you be my date for the semiformal?" she asked.

Neil heaved a big sigh of relief. That hadn't been so bad. "You bet," he said, yanking on the end of her ponytail.

Suddenly there was the sound of several feet shuffling outside the door and a series of long, loud knocks. "Hey, hey, party people!" a high female voice screamed. "Open up!"

Neil pulled back and looked at Jessica, cocking an eyebrow. "Friday during finals? Not even."

"Oh, um, yeah." A sly grin spread over her face. "I forgot to tell you. . . . We're, um, sort of having a wild party!"

Chloe, Sue, and the six in their group headed up the walkway to Jessica's house. Party time! Chloe could see through the bay window that there were people milling about the living room. And she could hear the faint sounds of music too. Tonight was going to be great!

"Chloe?"

She turned around at the unfamiliar voice. Looking at her hesitantly was a shy girl she recognized from

Oakley, the dorm she used to live in before she moved into Theta house. Jenny? Jenna? Something like that, Chloe thought.

Next to the girl was a semicute guy, tall with curly brown hair. Chloe hadn't gotten to know her too well; the girl was really shy. Whenever she saw her, she had her nose in a book. And now she was either on her way into the party or just passing by. In any case, she was actually talking now. Maybe a year of SVU had changed her too.

"I'm Jenna," she told Chloe. "You used to live in Oakley, right?"

Chloe held up her index finger, then turned to her group. "You guys go ahead. I'll see you inside." She turned back around to face Jenna with a smile. "Yeah. I live in Theta house now."

"Wow, that's so cool," Jenna said. "A friend of mine is in Theta, and she told me about this party, but I haven't seen her go in, so maybe she's not coming."

The guy next to Jenna coughed politely.

Jenna glanced at him. "Oh, sorry. Um, this is my brother, Luke. He's a sophomore."

"Hi, Luke," Chloe said with a smile. "I'm Chloe."

Luke smiled, and two amazing dimples formed on either side of his face. With his brown, curly hair and dark blue eyes, he looked like a younger version of Wes Bentley from *American Beauty*. *Cute*, Chloe thought. *Very cute.*

"So why don't you guys come in with me?" Chloe offered. "I'm sure your friend will show up sooner or later. Maybe she wanted to get some last minute studying in for a final."

Luke looked uncertain. "Are you sure? Sometimes it can be weird to go to the party you're invited to secondhand and the person isn't even there."

Don't I know it, Chloe thought. "I'm sure. It's no problem." Chloe surprised herself by stopping at that. Normally she would have gushed about knowing everyone who lived here and being invited personally by the queen of Theta.

"So you're a freshman?" Luke asked as they started up the walkway.

"My freshman days are over!" Chloe exclaimed. "I'm a sophomore-to-be."

Jenna laughed. "I know what you mean. I'm very ready not to be a freshman anymore. Hey, so are you going to the semiformal?"

Chloe blushed, then remembered that *not* having a date wasn't something to be embarrassed about. "Yeah. Stag."

"Maybe I'll see you there," Luke said. "I'm taking my lovely sister Jenna here, but, um, maybe you'll save me a dance?"

Chloe grinned. *I'll save you every dance!* she thought happily. "I'm gonna hold you to that."

Luke smiled back.

Chapter
Fourteen

Nina walked back and forth in her room, wondering where she could take her newly minted fashion-plate self. Starlights? No. She wasn't in the mood for a crowded nightclub. Yum-Yums was also out—she had drunk enough tall, skinny lattes to last her a lifetime. Jessica's party? Maybe. Perhaps if she showed up later, Elizabeth would be around. But what to do now?

Graham Rubin! Nina suddenly remembered her classmate's infamous Friday-night study sessions, held at his dorm room. They were a *must* for all the physics majors—all six of them, that was. Nina had attended only once, at the very beginning of her freshman year, and after being introduced to Tom, Dick, Harry, Moe, and Curly (or at least that was how Nina thought of them in her head) and their friends, she had scurried back to the library, convinced that quips about quarks and Vodka Vectors were not *exactly* her scene.

From her vantage point of two years, however, her fear over that particular social engagement seemed amusingly quaint, as did the get-togethers themselves. Did Graham still have them? Nina was sure that he did. In any case, it was long past time to find out.

Nina checked her reflection in the mirror, threw some gloss and keys in a bag, and headed over to Reid Hall, where she knew Graham lived.

She arrived at the dorm in minutes and found his name on the room list at the front of the hall. A quick elevator ride to the fifth floor, and in seconds Nina was knocking at room 519.

Graham opened the door himself. "Nina!"

Nina took a step back, then steeled herself and went forward. Around the room she saw many familiar faces, and the ones she didn't know *looked* familiar—typical physics-guy nerdiness.

"Nina!" went up in a chorus as she entered the room. Nina couldn't help smiling. They still remembered her! Curly—or the guy Nina called Curly—tugged on her elbow. "We thought you'd never come back," he said.

"It's great to see you!" Moe said.

Tom was standing by the drinks table and had

to shout across the room. "Hey, Nina, what can I get you?" he called.

Nina took a drink and sat down, overwhelmed by all the male attention. "So, what have you been up to, physics girl?" Graham asked.

Nina blushed and took a sip. Vodka Vectors weren't that bad, really—kind of like extra-sweet 7UP.

"Not much, really," Nina said. "How about yourself?"

Graham went into some long description about a robotics contest he was entering. The one he and his team were designing, he explained, didn't roll on casters—or rather, it *was* one big ball.

"But how does it accomplish anything, then?" Nina asked.

"Holes, m'dear," Graham said. "Vacuum suction."

Nina laughed. "Oh!" she said. "So it's like a big robot vacuum cleaner."

Graham looked thrilled. "Exactly!" he said. "Whaddya need a robot to bring you a drink for, that's what I want to know. Housework, that's the ticket." He gave a satisfied swallow. "We're working on a random dishwasher next."

Nina was completely relaxed and enjoying herself, she realized. This type of banter was much more her kind of thing than Starlights, which was a little too much for her system to handle. Here she didn't feel fireworks and karmic connections, but what had those amounted to in the end anyway? This laughter and conversation was a lot more real.

Nina was about to ask if Graham knew there already *was* such a thing as an automatic dishwasher when she caught the eye of a guy across the room. *Oh, no.* She groaned. *Not another one.*

The guy—who had clearly been eyeing Nina for a long time, she realized—was a tall, stunning, dark-haired hottie with a killer grin. As he caught Nina's eye, he grinned at her happily and raised his glass. Nina looked down hastily. *Don't look up now, Nina,* she coached herself. *You've been burned enough by those kind of guys.*

When she finally looked up again to start nodding back at Graham—now excitedly talking about some sort of rolling toothbrush and shower—she had to take a quick breath: The guy was standing right in front of her. He waited there until Graham finally noticed him and pounded him on the back.

"Hey, David," Graham said. "Have you met our glamour girl yet?"

"She strikes me as more than a glamour girl, mate," the guy quipped back in an unidentifiable accent.

That was new. Nina looked up. David's eyes

were a burnished steel gray, and he had a ready smile, evidently—not a self-satisfied smirk like Xavier. Where was he from? He sounded a little English, a little Australian. "What kind of an accent is that?" she asked.

"New Zealand, luv," David responded. "You know—straight into the sunset and left until morning."

Despite herself Nina laughed at the sudden reference to *Peter Pan*. David had the same kind of boyish grin—and boyish sense of humor, she realized. Hopefully he didn't have a boyish sense of romance as well—or a boorish one.

"David's a fellow in the philosophy program here," Graham said.

Ohhhh, no. Not another philosopher. "So you're majoring in philosophy?" she asked.

David flashed his white teeth. "Actually, I teach it," he said. "I took my Ph.D. at Oxford last year and got lucky enough to find this lovely position here. As well as other lovely things," he said, giving a funny sideways grin.

Nina's stomach flipped. Was he talking about her? *Glug-glug. Make conversation. And calm down.* "How did you meet Graham?" she asked, trying not to let her nervousness show in her voice.

"Oh, Graham and I teach a course together

here. You may have heard of it—Physics for Poets?" He smiled again.

Nina had heard of it—the course was designed for students who couldn't handle a lot of math but needed a science/math credit. It was sort of—the philosophy of physics, if such a thing could be said.

"Professor Montrose recommended me," Graham said, "when you weren't around much last term. But we'd love your help, Nina. Wouldn't we?" he asked David.

David's eyes snapped, and he patted Graham firmly on the back. "Wouldn't we!" he said heartily.

Nina smiled, having gotten back her poise while the boys were babbling. This type of thing she knew how to handle—stay aloof, but available. And see what happens.

"I'll certainly think about it," Nina replied. *Twenty-four seven.*

Todd practically skipped out of the dean's office, so filled with glee that he kept turning his baseball cap from the front to the back. He was in such a state of happiness that he almost bulldozed a group of familiar-looking girls.

"Chill pill, Todd!" Lila Fowler said snarkily. Denise Waters, Alexandra Rollins, and the usual cookie-cutter Thetas smiled at him.

"Oh, hey, Lila," Todd said. The last time he had seen her, he realized, was in the bookstore, where she and her friend had practically spit on him after they realized he was working full-time at Frankie's.

"How's the working life going?" Lila asked. Particularly nice for Lila, whose tongue could slice leather, Todd noticed. He'd expected another smart remark, but she looked genuinely interested. Could everyone—Todd suddenly realized—not have been looking down on him after all? Maybe they had just been a little *shocked*.

"Actually, I'm coming back to school." Todd gestured toward the building behind him.

Lila's eyes lit up. "Oh, really?" she asked. "When?"

"Monday, if all goes well." Todd was unable to keep from smiling like a goofy idiot. "Maybe I'll even go study tonight. Even though I don't have a class yet."

"Oh, you can't do that," Lila said, looking genuinely horrified. "There's a party at Jessica's. Everyone's going to be there."

I can go to parties now, Todd realized. *Just like a normal student, not a working stiff.* Maybe not tonight, though—he was still signed up to work.

"We'll see," he said. To his surprise, he realized he'd really like to see all of those people, even though he had been totally sick of them. Things changed fast when you didn't go to *extremes.* "I'll try anyway," he told her. "I actually gotta go back to work right now, though—I have to tell my boss what's happening."

"Be there!" Lila called over her shoulder. Todd nodded and grinned.

He caught a bus back to Frankie's. The forty-minute ride seemed to take even longer, of course, since he was bursting with information. Finally his stop. Todd jumped out and ran the two blocks to the bar, then went right to the back room, panting from his exertions, where he knew Rita would be sitting.

Before she could say anything, Todd launched into his spiel. "First of all, I have to tell you how much I appreciate everything you've done for me."

"Uh-oh," Rita said, taking her ubiquitous pencil out of her hair.

"But I've decided to go back to school full-time and pursue a degree in business management," Todd rushed out, breathless.

Rita nodded slowly. She didn't say anything for a couple of moments, but then she exhaled loudly. Todd braced himself for the onslaught.

"Well, we're sure gonna miss you around here," Rita said. "Me particularly, I have to say. But you know, I can't say I'm sorry to hear it."

Todd caught his breath. Could that be it? Maybe that last sentence was actually yelling at him somehow. "What do you mean?" he asked.

Rita smiled. "Well, you're a really smart guy and a hard worker, Todd. I guess I never expected to be able to keep you all to myself." She sighed. "I hoped to, though!"

Todd felt himself bursting with pride. "So you won't mind if I go part-time?" he asked.

Rita's eyes sparkled. "Remember that plan for you and Cathy to share the job of assistant manager?" Rita asked.

"Yeah," Todd said, feeling like everything might be okay after all.

"Well, why don't you train her this summer, and then we'll put it into action?" Rita said, tapping her pencil.

Todd could barely contain his enthusiasm. "Great!" he said.

"There's just one thing, though . . . ," Rita said, her face now somber.

"What?" Todd said. Was it going to be a pay cut? A lecture? Had he done something really bad?

"I'll still need your help with the ledger!" Rita exploded.

Todd began to laugh, loudly and deeply, half with happiness, half with relief. "No problem." He shook his head, tears coming out of his eyes. "No problem."

*   *   *

Elizabeth and Sam lay curled around each other on Elizabeth's bed, with only the moonlight coming in through the blinds. Sam gently kissed her on the forehead, and she felt like she might shatter into a thousand pieces. *It's right,* she told herself. *It's so scary, but it's right.*

They'd been up here now for about an hour, just lying together, kissing, caressing hands. She'd been wanting to say something all that time, something about how she felt. But the way they were touching each other seemed to speak volumes in itself.

She tried to tamp down her need to speak, but she couldn't finally. Egad—she was just going to have to tell Sam how she felt and try not to worry about it.

"I'm afraid to be honest with you about how I feel," Elizabeth whispered. "I'm afraid you're going to freak out on me and disappear again."

Sam was kissing her on her eyelids. Each kiss felt so exquisite, she felt like she might die with pleasure. At her statement he brought up his head and looked her in the eyes.

Sam sighed. "Talking about feelings isn't easy for me," he said. "But I want to make this work. You believe that, right?"

Elizabeth nodded and felt a welling up of joy and relief. *See?* She wanted to say to everyone and no one in particular. *I told you it would be all right!*

She smiled. She had never felt this relaxed and this turned on before—never in her life. She felt like a new Elizabeth was possible—a new Elizabeth that included the old one, not ignored her.

"I think I'll be ready soon," she whispered. "Soon."

Sam continued to kiss her all over her face. His hands on her back felt like some wonderful new sensation Elizabeth couldn't name—rolling in the waves or feeling the wind in her face. It was unbelievable. She began to kiss him and to let her fingers trail lightly down his back.

"Ready for what?" he whispered back.

She was totally surprised. He wasn't even thinking about it!

She smiled slyly at him. "To lose my virginity!"

She could feel Sam freeze completely. He drew back. "We have forever for that, Liz," he said earnestly. Elizabeth drew back too—was Sam's hesitation good or bad? Maybe he was really turned off by her.

"First," Sam said, looking into her eyes, "I want you to trust me totally. And we have all summer to work on that."

Elizabeth dissolved. She wanted to laugh and cry at the same time. Never before had she felt like a guy was speaking to her, for her, and not somehow trying to ignore her or to push her into something.

They were going to have the *best* summer.

Sam couldn't believe it! It had been only twenty-four hours, and already Elizabeth was talking about losing her virginity. Could this be the same girl he had lived with for this almost year?

He was going to have to put his foot down, or things were going to go much faster than he was comfortable with—emotionally, not sexually, he realized. *But I can do that, right?* Sam thought nervously. Looking down at the beautiful, incredibly wonderful Elizabeth, Sam could barely breathe. *Walk, don't run. Walk, don't run,* he cautioned himself, kissing the tip of her nose gently. *Or else you'll slip.*

Elizabeth sighed and turned over sleepily. Sam spooned her, breathing in the wonderful scent of her shampoo. After all this time he couldn't believe he'd been lucky enough to gain another chance, and with his arms around her, he couldn't imagine ever letting her go. Not while he was awake and breathing, that was for sure.

Committing himself to be her boyfriend was like getting on a roller coaster, he realized. Totally fast, thrilling, and disorienting all at the same time. And what did you have to do when you rode a roller coaster? Sam asked himself, gripping her in a fierce hug. *Just hold on tight and have fun.*

Jessica spun around, dancing an impromptu boogie with both Brett and Clyde at the same time. Neil was in the corner, talking to a very hot guy in overalls, but that was cool. She and her best friend were back in the black.

"Aiyaiyaiyaiyai!" Jessica screamed along with the music. She saw Elizabeth and Sam come downstairs, rubbing their eyes sleepily, looking confused to suddenly find half of Sweet Valley University in their kitchen and living room. "Hey, Lizzie," Jessica screamed, bounding over and giving her sister a big smackeroo on the cheek. Sam had his arm around Elizabeth's waist, Jessica noticed.

Uh-*huh*. So the famous Sam Burgess had managed to acknowledge a love greater than that of his turkey sub. Well, that was a step.

"You couldn't have mentioned it earlier?" Elizabeth asked, smiling wanly.

Jessica looked around innocently. "Mentioned *what?*" She saw Elizabeth's face break into a smile at the sight of Nina arriving with an incredibly hot dark-haired guy with broad shoulders.

"I'm going to say hi to Nina," Elizabeth said, kissing Sam on the cheek.

"I'm gonna call Bugsy and Floyd and invite

them," Sam said, dashing off to the phone. "It's been a while since they hung here."

Alone once again. Glad to know her *other* housemates were psyched to hang with *her*. "Oh, wait, Sam, they're already here!" Jessica called, but Sam didn't hear her over the din. He probably wouldn't appreciate hearing about the flight of fancy that had led her to go ahead and invite the two dumbbells when she inadvertently hit their number on the speed dial.

Suddenly she felt an arm grab her from behind. Neil grabbed her finger and dragged her across the party. "I want you to meet someone very special," he told her. Neil pointed her toward overalls man. "His name is Logan. And he's definitely gay."

Jessica smiled and began to tune out all the details of Mr. Wonderful, thinking about how wonderful it would be to find her own Mr. Wonderful. *Spring fever*, she thought. *Just a touch of spring fever.*

Jessica shook Logan's hand, then boogied away, leaving the two lovebirds alone. She smiled at Logan. She was so happy—all of her friends were in one room, finals would be over in mere days, and it would be summer. Beach, parties, swimming. Beach, lifeguards, parties. Beach, beach, beach . . . and boys. She couldn't concentrate, she felt so giddy.

Jessica noticed Lila, Alexandra, and Denise arriving; the room instantly parted for the Theta hotshots. Her heart bursting, Jessica practically flew over to her friends and grabbed them all in a big hug. Everyone had different summer plans, and come September, which seemed a world away, they'd all be juniors. Juniors. *Wow.*

Jessica hadn't made any summer plans beyond applying for the internship to that gallery. Maybe she'd get it. Maybe not. She'd probably work at Yum-Yums this summer, hang out with her sister—when Sam wasn't around, that was—and hang with Neil and his new love. Sounded pretty great to her. Jessica saw someone waving wildly to her; it was Chloe, smiling and dancing with a cute guy with curly brown hair.

It's been a great year, Jessica thought, dancing her way over to where Elizabeth was dancing with Nina. *And it's going to be an even better summer.*